MAUREEN SMITH

ROMANCING THE M.D.

KIMANI
ROMANCE

Special thanks and acknowledgment
are given to Maureen Smith for her contribution
to the Hopewell General miniseries.

For the men and women everywhere
who have devoted their lives to healing others.

My utmost gratitude to Zora Bilicich, who patiently answered
my questions about her native Colombia and provided the
Spanish translations for this book.

A heartfelt thanks to Sylvia Hightower, R.N.,
my go-to expert on all things medical.

 KIMANI PRESS™

Recycling programs
for this product may
not exist in your area.

ISBN-13: 978-0-373-86229-0

ROMANCING THE M.D.

**Tamara emerged from the hospital
to find Victor sitting astride a
gleaming black-and-silver motorcycle.
His long legs were covered in dark Levi's that
stretched taut across his strong, muscular thighs.**

Her mouth ran dry. "Victor."

"Hey, beautiful," he murmured. "Want a ride?"

She wanted a ride all right, but not necessarily the kind he was offering. She'd thought he couldn't look any sexier than he did in his scrubs, but damn, was she wrong. He looked hot as hell on his Harley, straddling the powerful bike with an innate, dangerous-edged masculinity that sent her hormones into overdrive. She wanted to hop onto the seat with him, thrust her breasts into his face and wrap her legs around his back.

"Let me give you a ride home."

She swallowed hard, shaking her head. "That's okay. I can walk."

"Why walk," he drawled, "when you can ride?"

Her bones turned to gelatin. "I only live fifteen minutes away."

"I'll get you there in five."

She glanced pointedly at the black helmet dangling from the motorcycle's handlebar. "You don't have one of those for me."

"Actually," he said, reaching inside a compartment next to the gas tank and producing another helmet, "I do." He held her gaze. "So let me take you home."

Tamara wavered, biting her lower lip.

"Get on, *cariño*." His voice dropped an octave, going indecently husky. "You know you want to."

Books by Maureen Smith

Kimani Romance

A Legal Affair
A Guilty Affair
A Risky Affair
Secret Agent Seduction
Touch of Heaven
Recipe for Temptation
Tempt Me at Midnight
Imagine Us
Romancing the M.D.

Kimani Arabesque

With Every Breath
A Heartbeat Away

MAUREEN SMITH

is the author of seventeen novels and one novella. She received a B.A. in English from the University of Maryland, with a minor in creative writing. She is a former freelance writer whose articles were featured in various print and online publications. Since the release of her debut novel in 2002, Maureen has been nominated for three *RT Book Reviews* Reviewers' Choice Awards and fourteen Emma Awards, and has won the *Romance in Color* Reviewers' Choice Awards for New Author of the Year and Romantic Suspense of the Year. Her novel *Secret Agent Seduction* won the 2010 Emma Award for Best Romantic Suspense.

Maureen lives in San Antonio, Texas, with her husband, two children and a miniature schnauzer. She loves to hear from readers and can be reached at author@maureen-smith.com. Please visit her website at www.maureen-smith.com for news about her upcoming releases.

Dear Reader,

I hope you've been enjoying the Hopewell General continuity series.

In the third installment, *Romancing the M.D.,* the scandal and drama continue with the story of rival interns Victor and Tamara. These brilliant cardiac surgeons share a sizzling attraction that they have been fighting for months. But even as they find themselves competing for the same research grant, they're already losing their hearts to each other....

It was fun for me to revisit Alexandria, Virginia, the setting for the fictitious Hopewell General Hospital. I grew up near Alexandria and worked in that lovely, historic city for three years. Victor and Tamara are about to create their own special memories there...if they don't kill each other first!

As always, please share your thoughts with me at author@maureen-smith.com.

Until next time, happy reading!

Maureen Smith

Romancing the M.D.
Glossary of Spanish Terms

Me importa un carajo—I don't give a damn

Vete al carajo—Go to hell

Cariño—Sweetheart (term of endearment)

Gracias—Thank you

Muchas gracias—Thank you very much

De nada—You're welcome

Mierda—Shit

Maldito sea—Damn it

Carajo—Damn it

Pendejo—Jerk

Vámos corre rápido—Let's go, run fast

Hermanote—affectionate nickname for an older brother (variant of *hermano*)

Culo—Ass

Muy bonita—Very beautiful

Mijo/mija—My son/my daughter

Papito—Daddy (often used as a Colombian term of endearment for sons)

Tía—Aunt

Apellido—Last name

Mira—Look

Bésame—Kiss me

Te necesito—I need you

Te adoro—I adore you

Te amo—I love you

No puedo vivir sin ti—I can't live without you

Quiero estar contigo para siempre—I want to be with you forever

Chapter 1

Dr. Tamara St. John was feeling murderous.

It was too bad she'd taken an oath to do no harm. Otherwise, Victor Aguilar García would be a dead man. A gorgeous one, but a corpse nevertheless.

They squared off in the hallway outside the room of a patient who'd been readmitted to the hospital after developing a postoperative wound infection. The two interns had struck combative poses, hands on hips, lab coats spread open as they argued with each other. Tamara hated that Victor's six-two frame forced her to angle her head back to meet his flashing gaze, and she hated that the dark blue color of his eyes reminded her of the most beautiful sapphire she'd ever seen.

"You're not listening to me," he said, the words gritted through straight white teeth. "Naphtomycin—"

"—is still in the clinical trial stage," Tamara interrupted

sharply. "So that means the jury's still out on the drug's safety and effectiveness. Unlike you, I don't like hedging my bets on a wildcard. I think we need to administer another course of antibiotics—"

"Because that's been working so well, right?" Victor countered mockingly.

Tamara bristled. "Let's not forget that this is *my* patient—"

"—who's been readmitted twice for a postoperative sternal wound that won't heal. It's time to pursue more aggressive treatment options."

"Naphtomycin isn't an option," Tamara said unequivocally.

"Well, it should be."

"I disagree. Until it's been approved by the FDA—"

Victor interrupted, "German physicians are already using Naphtomycin on their patients, with proven results."

"That doesn't matter," Tamara said obstinately.

"What do you mean it doesn't—" He broke off, shaking his head in angry exasperation. "Look, St. John, you have the potential to be a good cardiothoracic surgeon one day, but if you want to be the best, you're gonna have to start thinking outside the damn box."

"How dare you?" Tamara hissed furiously. "I don't need career advice from you! Last I checked, we *both* graduated from top medical schools, and we're *both* finalists for the same research grant—"

"Me importa un carajo!" Victor swore in Spanish, striking his fist against the wall. "Why does everything have to be a damn competition with you? This isn't about you and your egotistical need to be right—"

"*My* egotistical need?" Tamara sputtered in outrage.

"What about you? Every decision you make is based on the false assumption that you can never be wrong. You take risks with patients' lives like you're rolling dice on a craps table. Don't you *dare* lecture me about my ego when *you're* the one with the God complex!"

Victor scowled blackly. "I don't have a—"

"Like hell you don't!"

He glared at her another moment, then scrubbed his hands over his face and shook his head at the ceiling, as if he were petitioning God for a flood that would sweep her away. He needed a shave and a haircut, Tamara noted irritably, eyeing his stubble-roughened jaw and the thick dark hair that brushed his collar. He always looked like he'd just rolled out of bed, tossed on some clothes and hopped on to his Harley to ride to work. Tamara supposed that the rumpled, sexy look worked for some women. But not her. Everything about the man grated on her damn nerves.

She felt an unwelcome jolt as his strikingly blue eyes suddenly returned to hers. "Look, St. John," he said in a low, controlled voice, "I don't have time to stand here arguing with you, and the patient sure as hell can't afford any more delays in her treatment. Before you rule out administering Naphtomycin, just ask yourself what you would do if Mrs. Gruener were your mother."

"I wouldn't endanger her life by giving her a drug that hasn't even been approved by the FDA!" Tamara snapped.

"How do you know?" Victor shot back. "Until you're in that situation, you have *no* idea what measures you'd take to help your mother."

"I don't deal in hypotheticals. I deal with hard, cold facts, which is something you seem incapable of—"

"Why am I standing here talking to you?" Victor cut her off. "You're an intern just like me, so ultimately, it's not your call whether or not Mrs. Gruener receives Naphtomycin. And thank God for that!"

Tamara's eyes narrowed. "You wouldn't *dare* go over my head."

"Think I wouldn't? Let me tell you something. Mrs. Gruener's recovery is more important than your stubborn need to be right."

"You think I don't know that?"

"Sure as hell could have fooled—"

Beep, beep, beep!

The two combatants glanced down at the pagers clipped to their waists. When they saw the familiar code that signaled a crisis requiring all available medical personnel, they turned and rushed downstairs to the emergency room.

They were greeted by pandemonium as several stretchers bearing injured victims were wheeled into the hospital, where a triage had been set up to evaluate the new arrivals. Those who were most seriously injured were already being tended to.

Tamara and Victor hurried over to fellow intern Jaclyn Campbell, who was examining the bloody head wound of a teenager who was moaning in pain.

"What happened?" Tamara asked anxiously.

Jaclyn grimaced. "School bus accident. At least thirty students were on board, not to mention the driver and several other motorists involved in the collision."

"Shit," Tamara and Victor swore in unison.

"Let's go, people!" shouted Dr. Lucien De Winter, the new head of the E.R. at Hopewell General. He strode through the bustling emergency room, calling out authoritatively, "All hands on deck!"

Alerted by the wail of an approaching ambulance, Tamara and Victor raced outside to greet the arriving EMTs, who had just removed a stretcher bearing a teenage biracial girl covered with blood and multiple lacerations.

"She's hypotensive," one of the EMTs informed them as he and Victor quickly wheeled the gurney toward the entrance to the hospital. "Blood pressure's eighty-three over forty-two, pulse is one-thirty-six."

Moments after they rolled the new patient into the E.R., she went into cardiac arrest.

"She needs to be opened up!" Victor said urgently.

Tamara was already sprinting ahead, adrenaline pumping through her veins as she frantically searched for an attending physician to assist them. To her dismay, none could be found.

Victor and the EMT had wheeled the patient into an available trauma bay and were using a defibrillator on her. As Tamara raced in after them, Victor called over his shoulder, "We're gonna have to open her up!"

Tamara stared at him. "We can't!"

"Why the hell not?"

"We're interns, Victor! We're not supposed to be operating on patients!"

"If we don't help this girl ASAP," he barked, "she's going to die!"

Tamara knew he was right. The teenager had suffered blunt chest trauma during the traffic accident, so time was of the essence. Surely she and Victor wouldn't be punished for taking matters into their own hands in order to save the girl's life, she reasoned.

After casting one last glance around the chaotic emergency room, Tamara sprang into action, setting up the ultrasound machine as Victor hurriedly unpacked a tray containing the necessary equipment for an emergency resuscitative thoracotomy. They didn't have time to get the patient transported to an operating room. They'd have to perform the procedure right there in the E.R.

After intubating the patient and donning protective equipment, Tamara and Victor went to work cutting open her chest cavity to gain access to her heart. With the hospital's medical staff stretched perilously thin that morning, she and Victor had to rely on each other's training and instincts to ensure a successful operation. Like a precisely choreographed ballet, they passed the scalpel, scissors and forceps back and forth, and moved out of each other's way without being told. As Victor massaged the patient's heart with his gloved hands, Tamara murmured encouragements to him.

Suddenly their personal differences and grievances didn't matter. All that mattered was the single goal they shared—to save a young girl's life.

So that's what they focused on doing until an attending physician arrived to take over.

Later that evening—after their young patient had been transported to the intensive care unit for recovery, and the other accident victims had been stabilized or discharged—Tamara and Victor found themselves alone in the interns' locker room. It had been a long, exhausting day. All Tamara craved was a hot shower and a soft bed, though part of her was so wired from today's events that she wondered whether sleep would elude her tonight.

She was tying her sneakers when the deep, masculine timbre of Victor's voice came to her from the other side of the lockers. "You did a great job today."

Tamara straightened slowly from the floor. She was surprised by the unexpected compliment. And undeniably pleased.

"Thanks," she said. "So did you."

"Gracias." Victor paused for a moment. "We make a good team."

Something foreign fluttered in her belly. "Yeah," she agreed softly, "we do. Shocking, isn't it?"

He gave a low chuckle. "Yeah."

A long silence fell between them.

Tamara found herself holding her breath, waiting for him to say more. When he didn't, she rose from the bench, grabbed her backpack from the locker and swung the door shut. As she started from the room, she tossed over her shoulder, "I'll see you tom—"

"Wait up. I'll walk you outside."

She turned to watch as Victor emerged from behind the row of lockers. He'd changed into a blue T-shirt and dark jeans that rode low on his hips and clung to his strong, muscular thighs. His duffel bag was slung over his back, while a gleaming black helmet was tucked beneath his arm.

He sauntered toward her, exuding such raw magnetism that Tamara's mouth ran dry.

When he reached her, she noticed two things at once: the color of his T-shirt brought out the piercing blue of his eyes, and his hair had gotten tousled when he'd put on his clothes. She had an overwhelming urge to reach up and slide her fingers through the thick, wavy locks to see if they felt as soft as they looked.

"Ready?" Victor asked her.

She glanced away quickly. "Sure. Let's go."

They left the locker room and headed down the corridor toward the nearest exit. The hospital was so quiet, the chaos from that morning's school bus accident almost seemed like a distant memory. But Tamara knew she'd never forget it. She and Victor had saved a sixteen-year-old girl from dying today. No matter how many years she practiced medicine, or how many more lives she saved, Tamara hoped she'd never take a single miracle for granted.

As she and Victor neared the sliding glass doors that led to the parking lot, they saw that it was raining outside. No, not just raining. *Pouring.*

"Oh, no," Tamara groaned, dreading the fifteen-minute walk to her studio apartment in the torrential downpour. "I didn't bring my umbrella to work this morning."

"I don't think it'd do you much good," Victor muttered grimly, his heavy brows furrowed as he observed the slanted sheets of rain falling from the night sky. "You'd be soaked to the bone by the time you got halfway home."

"I know." Tamara frowned, eyeing the helmet under his arm. "You probably wouldn't fare much better on your bike."

"Probably not." But he looked like he wanted to try anyway.

She heaved a sigh. "This really sucks. I don't even remember the forecast calling for rain."

"I wouldn't know. I never listen to weather forecasts."

Tamara's mouth curved wryly. "Why doesn't that surprise me?"

Victor cocked a brow at her. "Meaning?"

"Meaning that you—" The rest of her reply was drowned out by a sharp clap of thunder that rattled the building and made the overhead lights flicker.

She and Victor stared at each other.

"Looks like we're gonna have to wait out the storm," he said.

Tamara nodded reluctantly. "Looks like."

Victor glanced around the quiet reception area, then said abruptly, "Come on."

Tamara frowned at him. "Where?"

"Just follow me." He started off down the hallway.

When she remained where she was, he glanced over his shoulder at her. "If anyone sees that we're still hanging around the hospital, we're gonna get drafted into pulling another shift."

He was right.

"Say no more," Tamara muttered, hurrying after him.

Chapter 2

They rode the elevator to the tenth floor, where they disembarked onto a vacant wing that was undergoing construction. The long corridors were dimly lit, and plastic tarp covered the dusty linoleum floors. With rain lashing at the windows and forks of lightning streaking across the sky, the empty ward had a decidedly gloomy atmosphere.

"We probably shouldn't be up here," Tamara said, her voice hushed.

Victor chuckled softly. "What's wrong? You afraid that some bogeyman is lurking in the shadows?"

"Of course not." A wry grin tugged at her lips. "But you have to admit that this *would* be the perfect setup for some cheesy horror movie. In fact, I'm pretty sure that Michael Myers has slaughtered more than his share of victims in deserted hospital wards."

Again, Victor chuckled. "Don't worry, *cariño*. I'll protect you."

Tamara forced herself to ignore the way her pulse skipped at the term of endearment, which he'd undoubtedly used without conscious thought.

As they walked down the empty corridor, their footsteps crunched against the plastic tarp, the sound echoing loudly in the silence. "Where, exactly, are we going?" Tamara asked.

"To find an open room."

"What if there aren't any?"

He slanted her an amused look. "Think positive."

They rounded a corner and tried the first door. It was locked, as were the next twelve doors they approached.

Weary and frustrated, Tamara was about to give up and suggest that they head back downstairs. And then they came to an unlocked room near the end of another hallway. Laughing softly, they slipped inside like a pair of vagrants relieved to find shelter on a brutal winter night.

When Tamara automatically reached for the light switch, Victor warned, "Don't turn it on, or someone might see us."

"Oops, that's right. I forgot."

Not that they really needed the light. Since the curtains were open, rooftop lighting from an adjacent building poured through the window to reveal a small room occupied by a single bed, a night table and a chair tucked into the corner.

It wasn't until Victor closed the door behind them that Tamara felt a moment's pause at being alone with him. Not because she was attracted to him or anything, she told herself. She just didn't want to be caught in a compromising position with him. Their chief of staff, Dr. Germaine Dudley, frowned upon intra-hospital relationships. The last thing Tamara needed was to be disqualified from receiving the research grant because she'd violated the hospital's nonfraternization policy.

"Make yourself comfortable," Victor told her.

She hesitated, then sat stiffly on the bed and shrugged out of her backpack.

Victor set his helmet on the table and dropped his duffel bag to the floor, then crossed the room to retrieve the lone chair. He dragged it over to the bed and plopped down with a grateful groan.

"Damn, it feels good to be off my feet," he said, stretching out his long legs and rubbing his hands over his face. "Thank God one of these rooms was open."

"Yeah." Tamara glanced out the window. "The rain doesn't appear to be letting up."

Victor followed the direction of her wistful gaze. "Nope. Looks like we'll be stuck here for a while."

She sighed heavily. "Looks that way."

Victor chuckled dryly, bending to remove his black boots. "Don't sound so depressed, St. John. I'm sure we can get through a couple more hours without killing each other. Especially if we're both asleep—which I intend to be pretty damn soon."

Tamara grinned. "Good point." After another hesitation, she toed off her sneakers, loosened her ponytail, then stretched out on the bed facing Victor. "We should probably set an alarm so we don't oversleep."

"Good idea." Victor pulled out his cell and quickly programmed some numbers, then stuffed the phone back into his pocket. "All set."

"Thanks," Tamara murmured.

"*De nada.* Sweet dreams."

"You, too."

She watched as he propped his big feet on the table, folded his hands across his flat abdomen, leaned back against the chair and closed his eyes.

Tamara rolled onto her back and stared up at the ceiling, willing sleep to come. But she was too keyed up to take a nap, and Victor's proximity didn't exactly help. It had been eons since she'd last gone on a date, let alone shared a bedroom with a man. And this wasn't just *any* man. This was her nemesis, her archrival, the only person who could derail her chance at landing the research grant she'd worked so hard to receive.

Gnawing her lower lip, Tamara cautiously turned her head on the pillow and looked at Victor, allowing her eyes to trace his features. Even *she* had to admit how ridiculously gorgeous he was, with thick dark brows, strong cheekbones, a square jaw and a deep, olive-toned complexion that was a gift of his Colombian heritage. But the feature Tamara found most distracting—next to his hypnotic blue eyes—were his lush, sensual lips. Watching those lips move had caused her to lose her train of thought more often than she cared to admit.

But she knew better than to indulge an attraction to Victor Aguilar, no matter how unbelievably hot he was. According to the rumor mill, he'd secretly dated over half the hospital's nursing staff, as well as one of their fellow interns, Isabelle Morales. Even if Tamara weren't a stickler for following rules, she wouldn't have allowed herself to become involved with Victor. Her sense of self-preservation was too strong for that.

So why are you lying here ogling the man when you're supposed to be sleeping? her conscience mocked.

Heat stung her face, and she quickly averted her gaze. As thunder rumbled outside the window, she squeezed her eyes shut and silently began counting sheep.

Several moments later she felt a light, prickling awareness that made her reopen her eyes and turn her head. Her heart thumped into her throat when she discovered Victor watching her from beneath the thick fringe of his dark lashes.

She stared at him.

He stared back.

After a prolonged silence, she whispered, "What's wrong?"

"Nothing."

"Can't sleep?"

He shook his head slowly. "You?"

She shook her head. "The thunder's too loud," she lied.

"Yeah." But he didn't sound very convinced.

"I think I'm too wired to sleep," she added, sitting up and folding her legs into a half-lotus position. "No matter how exhausted I am at the end of the day, it usually takes me a while to come down off an adrenaline rush."

Victor smiled a little. "Me, too."

Tamara hesitated, then said with soft wonder, "We performed an emergency thoracotomy today."

"We did, didn't we?"

She nodded. "Even though we were taught how to do the procedure in med school, we were always told that the survival rate is so low, less than two percent. But we beat the odds, Victor. We defied the experts, and Bethany Dennison lived. Isn't that amazing?"

"Absolutely," Victor agreed, gazing at her with an expression of quiet fascination.

She blushed, sheepishly biting her lip. "Sorry. Didn't mean to gush like that."

"Don't apologize. I feel the same way you do. That same sense of awe at the realization that you've been entrusted with people's lives, that all the education and training you've received comes down to that pivotal moment when someone's life hangs in the balance, and they're counting on you to pull them through." He paused, shaking his head slowly at Tamara. "It's powerful."

"Very," she whispered, shivers racing up and down her spine. She felt more connected to him than she'd ever imagined was possible before today.

They gazed at each other for several charged moments as lightning flashed outside the window.

A half smile quirked the corners of Victor's mouth. "Have you ever questioned your sanity for choosing cardiothoracic surgery as your specialty?"

Tamara grinned. "Why? Because we have to undergo four years of college, four years of medical school, seven years of a general surgery residency, and three more years of a 120-hour-per-week cardiothoracic surgery fellowship? *Nahhh.*"

Victor grinned. "Piece of cake, right?"

"Ab-so-lute-ly."

They looked at each other, then burst out laughing.

When their mirth subsided several moments later, Tamara let out a long, deep sigh. "Honestly? I *have* occasionally wondered whether I should explore a less demanding field, like dermatology or ophthalmology.

Something that would allow me to have some semblance of a life outside work."

"Marriage," Victor murmured. "Children. Guilt-free family vacations."

"Exactly," Tamara agreed. "I've never wanted to become one of those self-absorbed workaholics who's never around for my family, who's stuck in a hospital on gorgeous weekends while my husband and kids do fun things without me." She sighed. "On the other hand, I've always wanted to be a heart surgeon. The best of the best. I can't achieve that goal unless I'm willing to make some hard sacrifices."

Victor nodded slowly.

She knew he understood where she was coming from. They were both driven to succeed as cardiothoracic surgeons, who were considered among the most talented and sophisticated of their surgical peers. Not only were they required to master the field of general surgery, they also underwent extensive training, charted new areas of research and technology, and performed extremely dangerous and complex operations. Being a cardiothoracic surgeon was *not* for the faint of heart—no pun intended.

"So what about you, Aguilar?" Tamara ventured, turning the tables on him. "After a grueling eighteen-hour day, have you ever thought about throwing in the towel? Just surrendering your scrubs and walking away from the madness?"

He chuckled softly, dragging his hands through his thick dark hair. "Even if I ever wanted to quit, I have too many people depending on me not to."

"Your parents," Tamara surmised.

He nodded. "They came to this country with nothing

more than the clothes on their backs, and they worked their asses off to give me and my younger brothers a better life than the one we left behind in Colombia. I'm the first in my family to graduate from college. So my parents are counting on me to seize the American Dream so that I can reach back and help my siblings do the same thing. I'm not about to let them down."

Tamara gazed at him, filled with newfound respect and admiration for his loyalty to his family. At the same time, she was struck by the realization that they were halfway through their two-year internship, and she didn't know much about him.

She knew that he had at least one younger brother, who bore such a striking resemblance to him that Tamara had done a double take when she saw him. Alejandro Aguilar had stopped by the hospital one day to have lunch with Victor. Before they left, Victor had introduced his brother to Jaclyn and Isabelle, completely snubbing Tamara who'd been standing nearby, pretending not to notice or care.

Shoving aside the unpleasant memory of the slight, she asked curiously, "How many brothers do you have?"

"Four."

Her eyes widened incredulously. "Your parents have *five* sons?"

Victor gave her a crooked smile. "That's generally what four plus one equals."

"Shut up, smart-ass." But Tamara was grinning. "I feel sorry for your poor mother, being outnumbered like that."

Victor chuckled. "If you ever met my mother, you'd save your pity. She's always run the show in our family. Although my father would never admit it, we all know

Mama's the boss. So being the only female in the house has never made any difference to her."

Tamara smiled softly, enjoying this rare glimpse into his background. Although he was well liked and respected by their fellow interns, he'd been known to keep the details of his personal life close to the vest. Which was something else he and Tamara had in common.

"It sounds like you and your family are pretty tight," she observed.

"We are." A quiet, reflective smile touched Victor's mouth. "We've been through a lot together."

Tamara nodded, then couldn't resist asking gently, "Why did your parents leave Colombia?"

She watched as sorrow settled over his face like a veil. He looked past her, staring out the rain-streaked window. When he spoke, his voice was pitched low. "It was too dangerous to stay there. At the time, many parts of Bogotá were overrun with gangs. My parents lived in constant fear of something happening to one of us." He paused for a long moment, and Tamara instinctively braced herself for what he would reveal next. "One day, my uncle and his daughter were sitting on their front porch when a gunfight broke out between two rival gangs. They were killed in the crossfire."

A horrified gasp escaped Tamara's lips. "Oh, my God, Victor," she breathed. "How *awful*."

Pain flickered in his eyes. "That's the way it was," he said grimly. "Even if you were at home minding your own business, you could still be in the wrong place at the wrong time." His brooding gaze returned to Tamara's. "Not long after my uncle and cousin died, my parents packed up the family and fled to America, along with my aunt and her surviving children."

Tamara nodded, swallowing tightly. "Have you ever gone back?"

He nodded. "We still have many family members there. And I know it may sound hard to believe, but despite what happened, Bogotá will always be home."

"Of course. I understand." She shook her head mournfully. "I'm so sorry for your loss, Victor."

He inclined his head, silently acknowledging her condolences.

Neither spoke for a long time.

Seeking to distract him from his painful memories, Tamara asked softly, "Would you like a snack?"

Victor eyed her blankly. "A snack?"

"Yeah." She reached for her backpack and dug out a large plastic bag filled with an assortment of goodies. As she emptied the bag onto the bed, Victor lowered his feet to the floor and leaned forward to survey her stash.

"Whatcha got?"

Tamara grinned. "I got whatever you need, papi," she said teasingly, feeling like a drug dealer. "I got protein bars if you need a quick shot of energy, healthy granola bars if you feel like being good, and candy bars if you—"

She laughed as Victor snatched a Snickers out of her hand and tore open the wrapper. After taking a huge bite of the chocolate bar, he groaned appreciatively. "Mmm, that hits the spot."

Tamara *tsk-tsked* him. "I'm surprised at you, Dr. Aguilar, choosing empty carbs over more nutritious snacks."

"Says the woman with the bag full of candy bars," he muttered around a mouthful of chocolate.

Tamara grinned. "I only bring those to bribe the nurses into—"

"Bribe?" Victor interrupted in a tone of mock indignation. "Why, Dr. St. John, I didn't know you engaged in such unethical behavior. Shame on you."

Tamara chuckled. "Yeah, well, *some* of us don't have the nurses eating out of the palms of our hands. *Some* of us have to do more than wink and smile to get what we need around here."

Victor gave her a look of sham innocence. "I have no idea what you're talking about."

Tamara laughed. *"Riiight."*

Grinning, he polished off his Snickers bar and snagged another one.

She shook her head at him. "Keep eating all that junk and your arteries will get clogged, then I'll have to operate on you."

"Good."

"Good?"

He met her surprised gaze. "I wouldn't entrust my life to anyone but you."

Tamara warmed with pleasure at his words. "Likewise," she murmured. And she meant it.

Victor smiled at her, his eyes glittering like molten sapphires.

As they stared at each other, the moment stretched into two.

Glancing away, Tamara busied herself with returning the remaining snacks to the bag. "You know," she remarked offhandedly, "all the nurses think you look like Adam Rodriguez from *CSI.*"

"Yeah?" Victor drawled, leaning back in the chair and propping his sock-clad feet on the table as he continued munching on his candy bar. "And what do you think?"

She tilted her head to one side, lips pursed as she pretended to examine his masculine features. "I can definitely see the resemblance. But—" She broke off, shaking her head.

"But what?"

She hesitated, then sighed. "At the risk of further inflating your ego," she said grudgingly, "I think you're even better looking than Adam."

A slow, wicked grin curved Victor's mouth. "Are you flirting with me, Tamara?"

Heat rushed to her face. "Of course not."

"Are you sure? Because that would be against hospital policy, and you know—"

She rolled her eyes in exasperation. "I'm not flirting with you. Sheesh. Can't a woman compliment you without wanting to sleep with you?"

Victor looked thoughtful. "I don't know. I've never met one."

Sputtering with indignation, Tamara slapped his hard, muscled thigh. *"Pendejo!"* she hissed, seizing on her expanding Spanish vocabulary to call him a jerk.

He threw back his head and laughed, a strong, deep laugh that rumbled up from his chest and raised goose bumps along her skin. She'd have to be an occupant of the morgue not to be affected by his raw sex appeal.

"I forgot that you're learning Spanish from Isabelle so you can communicate with more of your patients," Victor said.

"That's right, and I'm a damn quick learner. So pretty soon I'll be able to insult you in *two* languages."

Again he laughed, discarding his Snickers wrapper in the trash. "You knew I had to say something to get a rise out of you," he teased. "We were getting along too well."

"God forbid we should do that," Tamara muttered, plumping up the stiff pillows before lying down on her side. "I'm going to sleep."

"You can't."

"Says who?"

"You have to keep me company until my sugar rush wears off."

She snorted. "No one told you to eat *two* candy bars."

"I had the munchies. Come on, Tamara," Victor cajoled, moving his foot from the table to playfully nudge her leg, a simple touch that sent heat crashing through her veins. "Keep me company."

"Fine," she relented with a huff, knowing damn well she wouldn't have been able to sleep anyway.

Over the next few hours, as the storm raged on outside, she and Victor talked and laughed, swapping horror stories from medical school and comparing notes on the best and worst professors they'd had. When Victor's cell phone beeped, he turned off the alarm and tossed the phone aside without missing a beat in their conversation. It seemed like they could talk all night and never run out of things to say to each other.

But eventually Tamara felt drowsiness settling over her like a warm blanket. Taking pity on Victor, who'd appeared increasingly uncomfortable in the chair, she invited him to share the bed with her.

It's just for another hour or so, she told herself as he stretched out alongside her, the heat of his body penetrating hers even though they weren't touching. *Surely it won't rain all night.*

Before sleep claimed her, the last thought that drifted through her mind was that after tonight, things would never be the same between her and Victor.

Chapter 3

Victor was having the most amazing dream.

It had to be a dream because he certainly didn't remember taking a date home last night, though it wouldn't be the first time he'd woken up in a woman's bed with no memory of how he'd gotten there.

But this time was different. The woman in his arms felt like she belonged there.

So she *couldn't* be real, his subconscious rationalized. He *had* to be imagining the gentle rise and fall of plump breasts, the tantalizing thrust of nipples against his chest, the shapely swell of hips beneath his hand, the luscious curve of a feminine thigh draped across his waist. She wasn't real, yet it seemed wholly natural for him to brush his lips over her forehead and nuzzle her soft, fragrant hair. And when she sighed contentedly and cuddled closer to him, he couldn't be blamed for the hot rush of arousal that sped to his groin and had him cupping the woman's lush, round bottom.

When she stiffened without warning, he snapped his eyes open.

And was greeted by the stunned, beautiful face of Tamara St. John.

They stared at each other in stricken silence.

An instant later they sprang apart, scrambling off the bed and facing each other from opposite sides.

"Wh-what happened?" Tamara whispered.

Victor, who could rattle off the most complex medical passages from the *Gray's Anatomy* textbook without batting an eye, suddenly found himself tongue-tied. "The storm... It was late... We, uh, fell asleep."

Their panicked gazes swung toward the window, where they could see the first blush of dawn breaking across the sky.

"When did it stop raining?" Tamara wondered aloud.

"I don't know." Victor paused. "I was asleep, like you."

"Oh, God," she groaned.

As she scurried around the bed to retrieve her shoes and backpack, Victor couldn't help thinking how exquisite she looked, with flushed cheeks and her dark, chestnut hair tousled about her face and shoulders.

She glanced up from tying her sneakers, eyeing him frantically. "Don't just stand there! Get your stuff so we can get out of here!"

Scrubbing an unsteady hand over his face, Victor shoved his feet into his boots and grabbed his duffel bag and helmet, then followed Tamara from the room.

When they reached the elevators, she said decisively,

"I'll go down first. We don't want anyone to see us leaving together at this hour."

Victor nodded. "Good idea."

They stood staring up at the electronic panel above the elevator doors, the air between them crackling with tension and bewilderment over this strange new territory they'd just wandered into.

"Tamara—"

"Victor—"

They spoke at the same time, then looked at each other.

At that moment, the elevator arrived.

Clearly relieved, Tamara boarded quickly and stabbed the down button as if she were fleeing the serial killer they'd joked about last night.

But as the metal doors slid closed, their gazes clung almost longingly.

That was the moment Victor realized that they could never go back to the way things used to be.

Thirty minutes later, he was still brooding over Tamara as he strode down a narrow hallway to reach his apartment. Just as he inserted his key in the lock, he heard the sound of another door opening just three doors away.

"Good morning, stranger," a sultry voice greeted him.

Victor glanced over his shoulder, meeting the sensual gaze of an attractive young woman with straight blond hair, perky breasts and long legs bared by the short skirt she'd donned for work that morning.

He flashed a lazy smile at her. "Hey, Natalia."

"Hey, yourself," she purred, lounging in the doorway of her apartment. "Every time I think I've got your schedule figured out, you prove me wrong. Did you work a double or triple shift yesterday?"

Victor chuckled. "No such thing as a 'triple shift.' Not technically, anyway."

She ran an eye over him, taking in his dark jeans and boots. "But you're just getting home from the hospital, right?"

"Right." He edged toward his door. "And I'm pretty beat, so if it's all the same to you—"

"How's your family doing?" Natalia interrupted.

He bit back an impatient sigh. "They're good."

"When was the last time you saw everyone?"

"Two weeks ago. But I'm hanging out with them this Sunday on my day off."

"That's great." Natalia sighed wistfully. "I really wish I could go with you, Victor. I adore your family, and I haven't seen them since…well, since we stopped dating."

Victor suppressed a pained grimace. He saw no reason to remind her that their "dating" had consisted of one take-out dinner and a few sweaty romps in the sack.

Natalia was the first person he'd met when he moved into the apartment building last year. She'd given him a friendly tour of the Alexandria neighborhood, followed by an even friendlier tour of her body hours later. With her long blond hair, green eyes and tanned curves, she looked like one of many California beach bunnies he'd encountered—and bedded—while at Stanford. So he'd been somewhat surprised to learn that Natalia was from his hometown, though he knew, of course, that Colombians come in all different shades. Upon meeting Natalia, his parents had also been pleased to discover that she was from Bogotá. They'd never made any secret of the fact that they expected Victor and his brothers to settle down with nice, respectable Colombian girls once they'd finished sowing their wild oats.

Natalia had thoroughly charmed Luis and Marcela Aguilar. By the time they left Victor's apartment that afternoon, they were practically planning his wedding. So they'd taken it especially hard when Victor informed them that he was no longer seeing his sexy neighbor. But he'd had no other choice but to level with them. He couldn't allow his parents to continue believing that he and Natalia had a future together when he knew better. He didn't have room in his life for a serious relationship. Completing his residency was priority number one, so he couldn't afford any distractions whatsoever.

After spending just one night with Tamara St. John, he already knew that *she* would measure an off-the-chart twenty on the Richter scale of distractions.

"Victor?"

Pulled out of his reverie, he eyed Natalia blankly. "Sorry. Did you say something?"

"Yes," she replied, looking slightly miffed at his inattention. "I was inviting you to dinner tomorrow night, if you're available. And I know that's a very big *if* given your crazy schedule. But if you have the night off, I'd like to have you over for dinner. I'll cook. You bring the wine."

Victor shook his head, smiling to soften his rejection. "Not that the offer doesn't sound tempting, but I'm afraid I'll have to pass."

"Are you working tomorrow?"

"I am." He paused. "But that's not the only reason I can't make it."

She sighed. "Just because we're not sleeping together anymore doesn't mean we can't be friends, Victor."

He gave her a skeptical look. "Is that what you want, Natalia? To be friends?"

"Sure, why not? We come from the same town. We live on the same floor. Your parents love me. We enjoy each other's company." She grinned slyly. "And if those aren't good enough reasons, we're great in bed together. So we could be friends with benefits."

Victor chuckled, rubbing his bristly jaw. "It's not that simple."

"Sure it is. Look, I'm making you an offer most guys would *kill* to receive. No-strings-attached sex and companionship. You want someone to vent to after a long, stressful day at the hospital? I'm your woman. You want a hot, delicious meal waiting for you when you get home? Look no further. You need to work off some pent-up sexual energy? I'm *all* yours."

Victor gave her a long, assessing look through narrowed eyes. "Why?"

She blinked. "Why what?"

"Why would you let any man take advantage of you like that?"

"You're not just *any man,* Victor. And you wouldn't be taking advantage of me, unless you honestly believe I'd consider it a chore to sleep with you." She smiled suggestively. "Trust me, I wouldn't."

Victor regarded her another moment, then shook his head and muttered under his breath, *"Mierda."*

Hearing the profanity, Natalia pouted. "So is that a no?"

"Absolutely."

"Are you sure?" She struck a seductive pose in the doorway, her mouth curving in a smile meant to entice.

But suddenly, all Victor could see were Tamara's alluring dark eyes, the plush softness of her lips, the smooth perfection of her deep brown skin, and the way her tight, shapely butt filled out her blue scrubs. It was crazy. Here he had a sexy, beautiful woman offering to cater to his every need, and all he could think about was some prickly smart-ass who'd hated his guts from the moment they met—and probably still did.

He needed to get his head examined by one of the neurosurgeons at the hospital.

Natalia heaved a lamenting sigh. "Well, if you change your mind about my offer—any of it—you know where to find me."

"Thanks," Victor drawled wryly. "I'll keep that in mind."

As he turned to unlock his door, Natalia let out a soft groan that drew his gaze back to her. She was grimacing as she massaged the back of her neck with one hand. "I don't know whether I'm stressed out from work, or I need a new mattress, but I've been having this *terrible* pain in my neck for weeks."

Victor's mouth twitched. "You should probably see a doctor about that."

She gave him a pointed look. "I've been *trying* to see a doctor, but he won't make any time for me."

"Hmm. Then you should probably find another one."

Chuckling at her disgruntled expression, Victor stepped inside his small apartment and closed the door behind him. After dropping his keys on the sideboard table and tossing his helmet onto the leather sofa, he started toward his bedroom. He wanted to take a hot shower and grab a few more hours of sleep before he had to return to the hospital that afternoon.

Ignoring the blinking message light on his phone, he headed into the adjoining bathroom and twisted on the shower faucet. The old building was plagued by bad plumbing, so he'd learned to give himself a head start if he wanted his water nice and steamy. Eventually, he planned to move into newer digs—someplace where he could actually enjoy hot showers that lasted longer than ten minutes. But for now, he was willing to sacrifice comfort for affordability and convenience. He'd gotten this apartment for a steal, so the money he saved went toward helping his family. Again, he had his priorities.

As he pulled off his T-shirt, his senses were filled with Tamara's sweet fragrance that clung to the fabric. She smelled like nectarines and warm, earthy woman. Unable to resist, he buried his nose in the shirt and breathed deeply, thinking he could get very addicted to the scent of Tamara St. John.

After several moments, he dropped the T-shirt on top of the wicker clothes hamper—in case he wanted to savor it again later—and finished undressing.

As he stepped inside the steamy shower stall and reached for a bar of soap, his thoughts remained on Tamara, replaying every moment of the night they'd spent together. He could still hear the smoky, bewitching sound of her laughter, could see the quiet wonder on her face as she'd recounted the experience of saving a young girl's life. He'd gotten chills when she spoke of her desire to become a cardiothoracic surgeon. The passion in her voice, in her glittering dark eyes, had struck a chord deep within him. He related so well to everything she'd said, he could have finished her sentences. Without intending to, he'd found himself sharing profoundly personal things with her, things that few people knew about him. But confiding in her had felt so right, as natural as them waking up in each other's arms.

Victor groaned softly at the memory of Tamara's lush breasts pressed against his chest, her curvy thigh hooked around his waist. She'd felt so damn good he'd thought he was dreaming. He'd wanted nothing more than to roll her onto her back, peel her jeans and panties off her legs, and bury himself deep inside her.

With another groan, he lifted his face to the hot spray of water and closed his eyes, conjuring an image of Tamara joining him in the shower. He imagined rivulets of water streaming down her beautiful brown skin, caressing the sensual contours of her body. He imagined palming her round breasts, teasing her dark nipples into hardened peaks. As she moaned with pleasure, he visualized his hand roaming down her sleek belly before he cupped her mound and slid two fingers inside her wet, succulent heat.

Caught up in the erotic fantasy, Victor reached down and wrapped his hand around his throbbing shaft. He stroked upward, then down, imagining Tamara's legs locked around his hips as he lifted her off the floor and pinned her against the tiled wall. As the warm water cascaded over their naked limbs, he imagined thrusting into her, her breathless cries soon mingling with his very real groans.

Throwing back his head, Victor fisted himself harder and faster until he ejaculated, his seed shooting out of him. Swearing gutturally, he bowed his head and braced his hands against the wall for support. As if on cue, the water turned cold, washing over his heated, shuddering body.

"Shit," he whispered hoarsely.

If fantasizing about Tamara could do this to him, he couldn't even conceive of what would happen if they ever hooked up for real.

He endured the frigid temperature for as long as he could, then staggered out of the shower stall and draped a towel around his hips. When his gaze landed on the T-shirt he'd left on top of the clothes hamper—the one that smelled like Tamara—he scowled. Stalking across the small bathroom, he grabbed the shirt, balled it up and shoved it deep inside the wicker basket.

The sooner he got the damn woman out of his system, the better off he'd be.

Chapter 4

That afternoon, Tamara met her mother for lunch at The Fish Market, an Old Town landmark perched at the end of Alexandria's historic King Street. Although the restaurant had devolved into more of a tourist trap in recent years, and the nautical decor was on the campy side, the place still served some of the best seafood in the area. Whenever Tamara and her mother were in the mood for crab cakes or greasy fish sandwiches, they knew where to go.

"Guess who I ran into yesterday," Vonda St. John announced halfway through the meal.

Tamara glanced up from a plate of pasta and scallops to meet her mother's gaze across the small table. "Who?"

There was an excited gleam in Vonda's almond-shaped eyes, which Tamara had inherited—along with her mother's high cheekbones, chocolate complexion, chestnut-colored hair and lithe, curvy physique. They looked so much alike that men often hit on them at the same time, claiming to mistake them for sisters. Considering that Vonda had only been seventeen when she gave birth to Tamara, it was no surprise that she looked young enough to pass for her twenty-six-year-old daughter's twin. But as close as she and Tamara were, there'd never been any question of who was the parent and who was the child. After Tamara's father skipped out on them, Vonda had dried her tears and staunchly committed herself to the task of raising a strong, fiercely independent woman who would never make the mistake of trusting the wrong man.

Tamara owed everything she was, and everything she would become, to her mother.

"Well?" she prompted when Vonda didn't immediately respond, no doubt trying to draw out the suspense. "Who did you run into?"

"Your high school sweetheart, Morris Richmond."

"Really?" Tamara exclaimed. "Where'd you see him?"

"At work."

"Morris works at the Pentagon, too?"

"As of last month. He got a job as a systems analyst for one of the defense contractors, and he's making good money." Vonda smiled at her daughter. "Of course he asked about you. I told him you're doing your residency at Hopewell General. He was very impressed, said he always knew you were going places. Don't be surprised if he shows up at the hospital one day. You wouldn't mind, would you?"

"Not at all," Tamara said easily. "I've often wondered how Morris was doing. It'd be nice to see him again."

Her mother grinned. "He's looking good, baby. *Real* good."

Tamara chuckled, sipping her cold soda. "I'm not surprised. He was one of the cutest boys at school."

"The smartest, too." Nostalgia softened Vonda's expression. "You two were such an adorable couple. I remember how Morris used to come over after school sometimes to study with you. I never had to worry about leaving you alone together, because you were both so studious and focused on your books. Acing your calculus exam was more important to you than getting inside each other's drawers."

"That's what *you* think." At her mother's shocked look, Tamara laughed. "Just kidding, Ma. We never abused your trust like that."

Vonda harrumphed. "I didn't think so. I raised you better than that, and Morris was such a sweet, respectful young man. I really liked him."

Tamara gave her a wry look. "Let's not forget that he's also the same one who broke up with me after I was named valedictorian over him."

"He did, didn't he?" Vonda pursed her lips for a moment, then shook her head. "It takes a very special man not to be intimidated by a strong, brilliant woman with a higher IQ. You're a force to be reckoned with, darling. Any man you eventually marry will have to be very successful in his own right so he won't feel threatened by you."

For no discernible reason, Tamara thought of Victor, who'd graduated at the top of his class from Stanford and seemed destined to make his mark in the field of cardiothoracic surgery. For all his faults—and he had plenty—Tamara knew that he would never feel threatened by a smart, accomplished woman. He was more than secure in his manhood, and would view someone like her as his equal.

Not that we're ever going to be in a relationship, she quickly told herself.

"So how are things going at work?" her mother asked, twirling strands of linguini around her fork before taking a bite. "What's the latest on the lawsuit?"

Tamara grimaced at the reminder of the hospital's brewing scandal. "They've hired someone from New York to handle the lawsuit—some hotshot lawyer named Maxwell Wade," she explained, though she and her colleagues had been instructed not to discuss the case with outsiders. But this was her mother, whom she'd always confided in. And details of the lawsuit had already been leaked to the media anyway.

"It sounds like your employer is going to need the best legal counsel money can buy," Vonda remarked.

Tamara nodded grimly. "They are."

After graduating from Dartmouth, she'd been so excited to return home to Alexandria to begin her residency at Hopewell General, a prestigious hospital that catered to the nation's power elite. But Hopewell's stellar reputation had recently come under fire after one of Tamara's fellow interns, Terrence Matthews, had been shown the door when he was caught stealing drugs from the hospital's pharmacy. Unfortunately, Terrence was a member of one of Virginia's wealthiest families, who'd retaliated against the hospital by withdrawing their financial support and filing a lawsuit. The public relations fallout and pending litigation had cast a pall over Hopewell General, putting everyone—from administrators to orderlies—on edge.

"The Matthews family is one of our biggest benefactors," Tamara continued, poking disinterestedly at her tender scallops. "Losing their financial contributions could really cripple the hospital. They've already halted construction on a wing that's been undergoing renovations for months."

Vonda frowned with concern. "What about your research grant? How will that be affected?"

Tamara sighed heavily. "I don't know yet. The hospital's funding committee is supposed to be meeting tomorrow to decide the fate of several projects, including the research grant. So I should know something by the end of the week."

Her mother reached across the table and patted her hand. "Think positive."

Tamara nodded, even as Victor's deep voice drifted through her mind. *Think positive,* he'd told her last night when they were searching for an unlocked room in the deserted ward. Since leaving the hospital that morning, she'd been trying to put the whole experience out of her mind. But she couldn't. Waking up in the arms of her nemesis shouldn't have felt so damn right. But it had, and she was afraid to examine why.

"No wonder you haven't been yourself today," her mother observed, watching as Tamara absently swirled her fork through a puddle of lemon cream sauce. "Ever since you arrived for lunch, you've seemed preoccupied with something."

Or someone, Tamara mused grimly.

"But your mood makes sense now," Vonda continued. "You're worried about losing the research grant."

"Well, technically," Tamara said ruefully, "I can't *lose* something I haven't received yet."

Vonda smiled indulgently. "I'm sure you're going to get the grant."

"I don't know, Ma. Victor has as good a shot as I do. His research related to cardiac arrhythmia surgery is pretty amazing. Potentially groundbreaking, in fact."

Vonda's sculpted brows lifted in surprise. "Are my ears deceiving me? Did you just say something *complimentary* about Dr. Aguilar?"

Tamara shrugged, feigning nonchalance. "I've said nice things about him before."

Vonda snorted. "Calling him an 'egomaniac,' a 'narcissistic asshole,' and a 'blue-eyed devil' doesn't exactly qualify as nice."

Tamara grinned sheepishly. "Okay, then. Let me go on record as saying that he's also a brilliant doctor, one that I admire and respect immensely."

Her mother stared at her for so long, Tamara was tempted to fidget in her chair the way she'd done as a child whenever she was caught doing something she wasn't supposed to.

As she watched uncomfortably, a slow, knowing smile spread across her mother's face. "Did something happen between you and Dr. Aguilar?"

Tamara's face flamed. "Of course not," she said quickly. Perhaps too quickly.

Vonda's eyes narrowed shrewdly on her face. "Are you sure?"

"Positive." It was true. Technically, nothing had happened between her and Victor—unless you counted talking the night away and waking up practically wrapped around each other. Her belly quivered wantonly at the memory of Victor's hand on her butt, his heavy erection pressed against her inner thigh. She'd tried to dismiss his hard-on by telling herself that he was merely experiencing nocturnal penile tumescence, aka the "morning wood" phenomenon familiar to most guys. But as she'd stood there facing Victor across the bed—trying not to notice how outrageously sexy he looked with his lids at half-mast, hair rumpled, jaw darkened with stubble—she'd been knocked breathless by the sudden realization that he wanted her.

And the feeling was unequivocally mutual.

Her mother studied her another moment, then reached for her margarita and took a long, deliberate sip.

Tamara waited.

Setting down her glass, Vonda said quietly, "Just be careful. You don't want to jeopardize everything you've worked so hard to achieve."

"I know," Tamara murmured. "Believe me, I have no intention of becoming involved with Victor Aguilar."

Her mother gave her a gentle, intuitive smile. "Sounds to me like you already are."

Shortly after Tamara and Victor reported to work that afternoon, they were approached by their supervisor, Dr. Shirley Balmer, who'd replaced Dr. De Winter as head resident. The attractive, forty-something woman bore such a strong resemblance to Angela Bassett that some of the interns often whispered lines from the actress's movies behind her back.

After ushering Tamara and Victor into the break room and closing the door behind them, Dr. Balmer demanded without preamble, "Whose idea was it to perform a thoracotomy on Bethany Dennison?"

Tamara and Victor exchanged glances.

"Why?" Tamara asked cautiously. "Is there a problem?"

Balmer's dark eyes narrowed. "Don't do that, Dr. St. John. Don't answer my question with a question."

"It was my idea," Victor said.

Balmer frowned, shaking her head at him. "Why doesn't that surprise me?"

"It was an emergency situation," Victor explained. "The patient had gone into cardiac arrest, and a judgment call had to be made."

"By an attending physician, Dr. Aguilar. Not by an intern."

"We couldn't find an attending," Tamara spoke up.

Balmer arched a dubious brow at her. "How hard did you look?"

At Tamara's hesitation, Victor interjected, "There wasn't enough time to go hunting someone down. The patient was coding. If we didn't act fast, she could have died."

"She also could have died as a result of a botched thoracotomy," Balmer countered, dividing a reproachful glance between Victor and Tamara. "Do either of you have any idea how much of a risk you took yesterday? As first-year interns, you lack the training and experience to operate on patients without supervision. If that girl had died, the hospital could be facing one hell of a malpractice lawsuit, and God knows that's the *last* thing we need right now."

Victor frowned at her. "Am I missing something

here? Did we, or did we not, save Bethany Dennison's life?"

"No one is disputing that, Dr. Aguilar. And I can certainly appreciate the difficult dilemma you both faced, having to weigh the risk of losing a patient against your obligation to follow standard hospital procedure."

Balmer paused, then heaved a deep breath. "Look, I know how anxious the two of you are to complete your internship and get into the nitty-gritty of practicing medicine. You both graduated at the top of your medical classes, and you're both overachievers. I sense your impatience every time you're restricted to suturing patients, Dr. Aguilar. And I know, Dr. St. John, that the field of cardiothoracic surgery is dominated by men, so you're eager to prove that you've got what it takes to hang with the boys. But you both need to understand that as exceptionally gifted as you may be, you still have plenty to learn about becoming surgeons. So just keep that in mind the next time you're faced with making a life or death decision. Are we clear?"

Tamara and Victor glanced at each other, then nodded dutifully. "Yes, ma'am."

"Good. Now get back to work."

As they moved toward the door, Dr. Balmer added, "Dr. Pederson, the attending physician who relieved you in the E.R. yesterday, was very impressed with the work you did on Bethany Dennison. He told me that some of his surgical peers have never even *attempted* an emergency resuscitative thoracotomy, much less succeeded at performing one. So congratulations to both of you. You've definitely gotten on the chief of surgery's radar."

Tamara and Victor grinned broadly at each other

before leaving the break room. Together they started down the hallway, enjoying a rare sense of camaraderie.

It was short-lived.

"Oh, before I forget," Dr. Balmer called after them. They glanced back at her, still smiling.

"I agree with Dr. Aguilar's recommendation to administer Naphtomycin to Mrs. Gruener. So I went ahead and ordered the course of antibiotics this morning." Balmer looked at Tamara, brow arched. "I assume that's okay with you, Dr. St. John?"

Tamara frowned. "Actually, I'm concerned that—"

Balmer's pager went off. After checking the display screen, she muttered, "Duty calls," then turned and hurried off in the opposite direction.

Tamara glared accusingly at Victor. "I can't believe you went behind my back and talked to Dr. Balmer."

He scowled. "You didn't leave me any other choice. You refused to see reason—"

"*Reason?* Do you honestly think there's anything reasonable about prescribing an unproven, potentially harmful drug to a seventy-five-year-old woman?"

"I do." Victor paused. "And, obviously, so does our supervisor."

Tamara's temper flared. "For Mrs. Gruener's sake, I hope to hell you're both right."

And with that, she stalked off down the hall.

Chapter 5

Over the next three days, Tamara and Victor went to great pains to try to avoid each other. If Tamara entered the on-call room where Victor was napping on the bottom bunk bed, she turned and hurried back out the door. If Victor strode into the cafeteria and saw Tamara seated alone at a table, he acknowledged her presence with a brusque nod and kept walking. They were constantly on the move—examining patients, reviewing charts, dispensing prescriptions, rushing into emergencies to save the sick and dying. Yet they were part of a team, so try as they might, it was impossible for either of them to pretend the other didn't exist.

On Friday afternoon, they were summoned to the chief of staff's office to learn the fate of the research grant they were both vying for. They sat stiffly beside each other as Dr. Dudley informed them that the hospital's grant committee had decided to put a freeze on all funding projects pending the outcome of the Matthews lawsuit.

"I know you're both disappointed," Dr. Dudley said at the end of his spiel, "and I wish I had better news to share with you at this time. But, unfortunately, none of us could have foreseen the unsavory circumstances that would befall the hospital."

"Of course," Tamara murmured, injecting an appropriate amount of deference into her voice. "We understand."

"Speak for yourself," Victor said shortly.

Both Tamara and Dr. Dudley stared at him in surprise.

"I beg your pardon?" the chief of staff demanded imperiously.

"With all due respect, sir," Victor said, leaning forward in his chair as he pinned the older man with a direct gaze. "I don't understand why funding for the research grant has to be postponed. I mean, I realize that this frivolous lawsuit has everyone shaking in their boots—"

"Dr. Aguilar—"

"—but let's be honest here. This hospital rakes in millions a year in financial donations. We treat senators and media moguls and insanely rich philanthropists. Our mission statement boasts that we're on the cutting edge of medicine. Dr. St. John and I are each working on important research that could save countless lives and bring even more prestige to this institute. But we can't do it on a shoestring budget. We need more funding in order to continue our work. But I guess it shouldn't surprise me that a bunch of bureaucrats fail to grasp that basic concept."

"Dr. Aguilar," the chief of staff blustered indignantly, "you are way out of line! You may not agree with the committee's decision, but you'll damn well respect it. Furthermore, you and Dr. St. John are more than welcome to explore other funding sources. There are a number of organizations and societies—"

"I know." Victor's cool, narrow smile reeked of belligerence. "I guess I was just hoping that the hospital would honor its commitment to always put patient care above bureaucracy, which is what we were all promised upon acceptance into the residency program. But I guess some promises aren't worth keeping around here."

Face suffused with outrage, Dr. Dudley jabbed a warning finger at Victor. "Now you listen here—"

Tamara jumped out of her chair. "Goodness, where has the time gone?" she exclaimed, making an exaggerated show of checking her watch. "I really hate to cut and run, Dr. Dudley, but Victor and I have another meeting to attend, and Dr. Balmer doesn't tolerate tardiness. So—" she grabbed Victor's rigid arm and tugged him to his feet "—we're just going to go and leave you to your work. We know what a busy man you are."

"Yes, I am." Dr. Dudley glared reproachfully at Victor, whose expression had turned downright surly. "You may be a gifted doctor, Aguilar, but you've got a hell of a lot to learn about organizational structure."

Before Victor could open his mouth to respond, Tamara smoothly interjected, "He'll take that under advisement, sir. Thank you." And with that, she ushered Victor out of the office, which was about as easy as dragging a wild stallion up a rocky gorge.

Once they left the outer reception area occupied by Dr. Dudley's assistant—whose mouth was agape—Victor shook off Tamara's hold and stalked off down the corridor.

She marched after him, seething with frustration. Reaching him at the elevator, she burst out incredulously, "Have you lost your damn mind? What the hell's gotten into you, talking to Dudley like that?"

"Vete al carajo," Victor muttered darkly, stabbing the elevator button.

"What? Did you just tell me to go to hell?"

"Damn right I did," he growled, rounding furiously on her. "And let's get something straight right now. I'm not a damn child who needs to be censored. I meant every word I said to Dudley, so I don't need you to intervene on my behalf!"

"Are you serious? You should be thanking me!"

"Thanking you!" he repeated, his thick brows slamming together over his flashing eyes. "What the hell should I thank you for?"

"I just saved your ass in there! In case you've forgotten, Dr. Dudley is the chief of staff. After the way you just mouthed off to him, he could kick you out of the program!"

Victor scowled. "Like *you* give a damn."

"I *don't* give a damn," Tamara shot back. "But if you want to torpedo your own career, I'd rather not be a witness to the spectacle!"

"Oh, I'm sorry," Victor jeered sarcastically. "Did I offend your conformist sensibilities?"

"Conformist?" Tamara sputtered in outrage.

"You heard me. You never push back or rock the boat. You swallow whatever crap they feed you like the good little soldier you are."

"Just because—" Tamara was interrupted by a discreet chime that announced the arrival of an elevator. She and Victor stomped inside, squaring off across the confined space as she continued furiously, "Just because I don't throw temper tantrums when I don't get my way doesn't mean I'm a conformist. I'm just as disappointed as you are that neither of us is getting the funds for the research grant, but I'm smart enough to know that antagonizing Dudley isn't the way to go about—"

"Maldito sea!" Victor exploded, cutting her off with a disgusted wave of his hand. "Can you really be this naive? They've been trying to cut back on costs for months, and this lawsuit just gave them a convenient excuse to do so!"

Tamara gaped at him. "You can't be serious! Are you actually suggesting that they're *happy* about this lawsuit? The Matthews family is dragging the hospital's name through the mud and withdrawing their financial support. In what alternate universe is that a *good* thing?"

"I'm not saying they're happy about the damn lawsuit," Victor ground out through tightly clenched teeth. "I'm saying that they're capitalizing on their misfortune at the expense of advancing medicine."

Tamara scowled impatiently. "What part of 'putting a freeze on funding' did you not understand? They didn't say we're never getting the money. They're just postponing the funding until the lawsuit has been resolved."

"Do you have any idea how many years that could take? Do you have the slightest clue how long this hospital could be tied up in litigation?" Victor shook his head at her, torn between incredulity and exasperation. "My God, you're naive."

Tamara bristled. "I'm not naive!"

"The hell you aren't!"

They didn't even realize that the elevator had reached their floor until the doors opened and an amused voice intoned dryly, "Uh-oh. The Bickersons are at it again. We'd better wait for the next one."

Tamara and Victor didn't bat an eye as the doors slid closed, leaving them alone like two heavyweight boxers slugging it out inside a ring. Intent on finishing their heated bout, Victor punched a random button, setting the elevator in motion again.

"I am so sick and tired of your maverick bullshit," Tamara snarled, enunciating each word with a sharp poke to his muscled chest. "I'm tired of the way you saunter around here thinking that you're smarter than everyone, that you have all the answers—"

"And *I'm* tired of dealing with a Goody Two-shoes who can't take a shit without making sure it's done by the book," Victor snarled back, eyes glittering with fury as he got in her face. The heat between them was scorching enough to set the entire building ablaze.

Heart pounding erratically, Tamara glared up at him, eyes narrowed to cold slits. "It would serve you right if Dudley tossed you out on your ass."

Victor laughed caustically. "Funny that you should mention *my* ass, when yours is the one Dudley couldn't take his eyes off as you left the room. But you were so busy trying to rescue me from myself that you didn't even notice."

Heat stung her face. "You think I give a damn about that?" she fired back. "Everyone knows what a total lech Dudley is. But what does that have to do with you being a complete jack—"

Without warning, Victor caught her face between his hands and crushed his mouth to hers.

She gasped, and instinctively grabbed for his arms. As his thick, hard muscles flexed beneath her palms, she tried to summon the willpower to push him away. But she couldn't. Not right then. His lips were so soft and warm, more temptingly lush than any man's had a right to be.

She trembled as his tongue snaked out and traced her lips, then plunged inside her mouth with a demanding hunger that left her senses reeling. As he stroked and sucked her tongue, arousal pounded between her thighs, wetting her panties.

Another moment of this, and she'd be begging Victor to screw her right where they stood, consequences be damned.

Stricken at the thought, she wrenched her mouth from his and stumbled backward, staring at him in stunned disbelief.

Something like guilt flickered in his smoldering eyes. "I'm sor—"

She slapped him across the face. "Don't you *ever* do that again," she hissed.

They glared at each other, the air between them charged with an explosive combination of anger, hostility and raw animal lust.

When the elevator stopped on an empty floor, Victor growled, "I'll take the stairs."

Tamara watched him stalk off down the hallway. As soon as the elevator doors closed, she brought trembling fingers to her swollen lips and sagged weakly against the wall. Her nipples were hard, and her clit was throbbing so violently she felt the reverberations in her skull. She couldn't have been more shaken than if an earthquake had rattled the ground beneath her feet.

"Dear God," she whispered.

She'd survived the desertion of her father, and the years of poverty and uncertainty that had followed. She'd survived being hospitalized after a common cold worsened into life-threatening pneumonia. She'd even survived the rigors of medical school, and was coping with the stressful, grueling eighteen-hour days demanded of her.

But after everything she'd been through and had successfully conquered, it staggered Tamara to realize that her downfall might ultimately come in the form of a tall, dark, blue-eyed devil.

Chapter 6

"Is it true?"

Victor glanced up from the discharge summary he'd been working on to watch as one of his fellow interns, Ravi Patel, sat across the table from him.

It was Saturday afternoon. After making his morning rounds and ordering lab tests for two patients he suspected of having coronary artery disease, Victor had grabbed some paperwork and headed outside to the hospital's landscaped courtyard to enjoy something he rarely experienced anymore—daylight.

He frowned at Ravi. "Is what true?"

"Did you get into an argument with Dr. Dudley yesterday?"

Victor grimaced. No wonder he'd been getting strange looks from his colleagues all morning. "Where'd you hear that?" he asked warily, though he could take an educated guess.

"Dr. Dudley's assistant has been telling everyone that you told him off, accused him of withholding money for a grant and called him a bureaucrat right to his face. Is that true?"

"Mierda," Victor muttered, tossing down his pen and scrubbing a hand over his face.

"Holy shit!" Ravi exclaimed, staring at him with an expression of awe and incredulity. "You really *did* say those things?"

"Yeah."

Ravi grinned broadly, his teeth flashing white against his dark skin. "You're crazy, man. Dr. Dudley's the chief of staff. *No one* talks to him like that."

"I know," Victor said darkly. "Believe me, I've already heard more than an earful."

"His assistant says he was royally pissed for the rest of the day. He even told Dr. Balmer that he's thinking about taking disciplinary action against you."

Victor blew out a deep, ragged breath and shoved his hands through his hair. "Great."

Ravi's grin widened. "I don't know if telling him off was the smartest thing you've ever done, Aguilar, but I definitely admire your *cojones*. You've got some brass ones."

"For all the good they'll do me," Victor grumbled.

Ravi laughed, shaking his head. "Here's my suggestion. If Dudley threatens to bounce you out of the residency program, just tell him you'll sue the hospital like Terrence did, and that should make him back off."

Victor smiled grimly. "Thanks for the advice, counselor."

"Anytime." Leaning back in the chair, Ravi pushed his wavy black hair off his forehead. The gesture reminded Victor of Dr. Balmer's running commentary about him and Ravi needing haircuts.

"So what's going on between you and Tamara?" Ravi asked abruptly.

The question caught Victor off guard. He stared at his colleague. "Nothing," he lied automatically. "Why?"

Ravi gave him a knowing look. "Come on, man. You don't think anyone has noticed the way you and Tamara have been acting this week?"

"We've hardly even been around each other."

"Exactly. It's like you've both been going out of your way to avoid each other. And then yesterday, Jaclyn and Isabelle overheard you two arguing on the elevator. They said you didn't even notice them standing there."

Victor scowled. "Don't you people have better things to do than gossip about your fellow interns?"

Ravi grinned unabashedly. "What can I say? We have to have *something* other than Terrence's lawsuit to talk about. And quite frankly, you and Tamara are far more interesting."

"Why?" Victor groused. "Because we were caught arguing? That's nothing new."

Ravi gave an amused snort. "Tell me about it. Why do you think we call you two the 'Bickersons'? You're always at each other's throats." He paused, a note of sly insinuation entering his voice. "It kinda makes some of us wonder…"

Victor didn't want to ask, but he had to know. "Wonder what?"

"Well, you know how the saying goes. There's a thin line between love and hate."

Victor swallowed hard, thinking of the brief but explosive kiss he and Tamara had shared yesterday. Or, rather, the kiss he'd stolen from her. He couldn't help himself. Arguing with the damn woman turned him on like nothing he'd ever encountered before. One moment he'd want to throttle her. The very next moment, he'd be struck with a fierce, powerful urge to haul her into his arms and kiss her senseless. So that's what he'd done. And she'd felt and tasted so good, he'd nearly lost control of himself. If that kiss had lasted a second longer, he would have lowered her to the floor or taken her against the wall—whichever got him inside her faster.

Last night he'd lain awake for hours, his body burning with lust as he tortured himself with mental replays of the steamy encounter. As he fought the urge to get himself off again like some horny adolescent, he'd thought of Natalia's offer to help relieve his pent-up sexual energy. He knew that, even at three in the morning, he would have been welcomed into her bed. But even if he'd been willing to use Natalia that way— which he wasn't—he knew that no other woman could satisfy his craving for Tamara.

Ravi was watching him intently, a speculative gleam in his black eyes. "So you're sure there's nothing going on between you and Tamara?"

"Of course I'm sure," Victor muttered darkly, grabbing his ballpoint pen to signal that the conversation was over. "So spread the word."

"Okay." Ravi heaved an exaggerated sigh of regret. "But the others will be sorely disappointed, and not just because they're looking for something other than the lawsuit scandal to gossip about."

A wry, indulgent smile quirked one corner of Victor's mouth. "And why will they be disappointed?"

Ravi shrugged. "Despite the way you and Tamara bicker all the time, some of us think you might actually make a good couple. You know, because opposites attract and all that." He paused. "But what do we know, right?"

Victor just stared at him.

Ravi grinned. "Well, I'd better get back inside and check on some patients. Unlike you, I wasn't smart enough to bring paperwork outside." He stood, clapping Victor on the shoulder. "Stay out of trouble, my friend."

Famous last words, Victor mused grimly as he returned to the discharge summary he'd been drafting for a patient who'd been sent home yesterday after being treated for congestive heart failure. Most interns loathed having to write discharge summaries, but since the reports were a necessary evil, Victor was learning how to make his as concise as possible.

But his concentration was shot, and before long he found himself lifting his head and idly glancing around. From the courtyard he had an unobstructed view of the front parking lot. When he spied Tamara walking toward the main entrance of the hospital, his pulse thudded.

She wore a fitted skirt that showed off a pair of toned, curvy legs that made him salivate even from this distance. After months of working with her, he knew that she preferred wearing ponytails, which she usually assembled as soon as she'd finished changing into her scrubs in the locker room. But for now her hair was loose, the dark strands lifting in the breeze to caress her face. Victor thought she looked radiantly beautiful.

Only problem was, she wasn't alone.

Walking beside her was a tall, brown-skinned man with a clean-shaven head.

Victor clenched his jaw, his gut tightening as he watched the couple stroll across the parking lot. He couldn't help but notice how relaxed they seemed with each other, like a pair of old friends or reunited lovers. When the man leaned down and murmured something in Tamara's ear, she threw back her head and laughed.

Victor felt a sharp stab of jealousy that surprised him. He had no reason to feel possessive over Tamara. They weren't dating, and probably never would be. Yet seeing her with another guy rubbed him the wrong way. And that was putting it mildly.

He glared as Tamara and her companion headed into the building.

And then he gathered up his paperwork and followed suit.

"So who was that fella you brought to work this afternoon?"

Tamara glanced up from reviewing patient charts to meet the inquisitive gaze of the forty-something redhead manning the nurses' station. She smiled wryly. "Does anything get past you, Sheryl?"

"Nope. I've got spies all over this place." The woman grinned unabashedly, her green eyes twinkling with mischief. "Jerome happened to be downstairs when you and your mystery man strolled through the lobby earlier. Jerome told me he walked you to the elevator and kissed you on the cheek like you were ending a date."

Tamara chuckled, shaking her head at the mention of Jerome Stubbs, a male nurse whose infectious sense of humor had made him popular with most of the staff. He also had a penchant for getting the scoop on any brewing scandals at the hospital.

"It wasn't really a date," Tamara said, uncomfortable, as always, with discussing her personal life at work. "We just went somewhere for breakfast."

"Sounds like a date to me." Sheryl Newsome leaned forward, eyes alight with avid curiosity. "So who was he?"

Tamara hesitated, silently cursing Morris's insistence on walking her inside the hospital. She should have known that one of her colleagues would see them and speculate about the nature of their relationship. But she hadn't wanted to hurt Morris's feelings by rejecting his chivalrous offer. She'd been pleased when he called two days ago and asked her out. Although she knew she had no room in her life for romance, she'd looked forward to catching up on old times with Morris. And she'd been secretly hoping that going out with him would, at least, take her mind off Victor for a while. But no such luck. She'd found herself thinking about Victor over breakfast with her ex-boyfriend. Which was really a shame, because Morris was smart, handsome and a great conversationalist, and she'd genuinely enjoyed his company. But she'd felt no spark of attraction for him. Whatever chemistry they'd shared as teenagers was long gone.

At the end of the meal when Morris asked her out again, Tamara had been honest with him, gently telling him that they could be friends, but nothing more. The last thing she wanted to do was lead him on.

"Well?" Sheryl prompted, watching Tamara expectantly. "Are you gonna give up the goods or what?"

Tamara sighed, rolling her eyes in mock exasperation. "Since you insist on being all up in my business—"

Sheryl grinned. "I do."

"—his name's Morris Richmond. We dated in high school."

"Ohh, how adorable," Sheryl cooed. "Your high school sweetheart. You should have brought him upstairs and introduced him to everyone. Right, Victor?"

Tamara stiffened, then reluctantly turned around to watch as her nemesis joined her at the nurses' station. As usual, his hair looked like he'd been running restless fingers through it, and at least five days' worth of stubble darkened his square jaw. He was sexier than any man had a right to be, damn him.

"Dr. Aguilar," Tamara said coolly.

He inclined his head. "Dr. St. John." Setting a folder down on the counter, he asked Sheryl, "What were you asking me?"

The nurse grinned. "I was just telling Tamara that she should have introduced us to her date. I don't know about you, but I'd love to see what her type is."

"Hmm," Victor murmured, his hooded eyes probing Tamara's. "That *would* be interesting."

She flushed, averting her gaze to look at Sheryl. "I don't have a type."

"Come now," Victor drawled with lazy insolence. "Everyone has a type."

Tamara smirked at him. "*You* don't, apparently."

Sheryl burst out laughing. "She's got you there, Dr. *Caliente*."

Victor scowled. "Yeah, whatever."

Grinning, Sheryl wagged her head at him. "Are you finished with Mr. Armstrong's chart?"

"Finishing it now," Victor muttered, removing a pen from the pocket of his lab coat and opening his folder.

"Take your time, honey." Sheryl propped her chin on her hand and smiled up at Tamara. "So where did Morris take you for breakfast? Not some coffee shop, I hope?"

"No," Tamara said with a chuckle. "We went to the Carlyle in Arlington."

"Ooh. Very nice," Sheryl said approvingly. "I've heard nothing but good things about that place."

"I can definitely see why. It's a great restaurant, kind of upscale. Brunch is really their specialty."

"That's what I've been told. So what'd you have?"

"The brioche French toast. Mmm-mmm. And their mimosas are delicious, too."

"You drank alcohol before coming to work, Dr. St. John?" Victor drawled without glancing up from his paperwork. *"Tsk tsk."*

Tamara shot him a withering look. "I had *one* glass."

"Still. You're a doctor. I'm surprised that you would take such a risk."

Tamara took umbrage, incensed by the suggestion that she would deliberately endanger patients' lives. "Why don't you just mind your own business?"

"We're a team," he countered evenly. "So, technically, everything you do around here *is* my business."

"Oh, yeah?" she flung back. "Since when did *you* become the resident narc?"

"Whoa, Bickersons," Sheryl intervened, making a timeout gesture with her hands. She divided an exasperated look between them. "Sheesh. Can't you two ever give it a rest?"

"He started it," Tamara snapped.

Victor smirked. "Real mature."

"*You* should talk."

To circumvent another quarrel, Sheryl quickly interjected, "Finish telling me about your date, Tamara."

Temper simmering, she forced a bright smile. "We had a wonderful time. Morris is a real gentleman who knows how to treat a woman. Honestly, he's as sweet and charming as he was back in high school. And since he remembered how much I used to enjoy watching plays, he invited me to—"

"Damn, my pen's out of ink," Victor muttered, lifting his head from his paperwork. He glanced at Tamara. "Excuse me."

Her pulse went haywire as he leaned past her to retrieve another ballpoint from the pen holder on the counter beside her. When his arm lightly grazed her breasts, her nipples hardened. As she tried to move out of his way, their eyes caught and held. Her heart rate quadrupled.

After a prolonged moment, his gaze lowered to her mouth. By the way his pupils darkened, Tamara could tell that he was remembering the scorching kiss they'd shared in the elevator. It was all she'd been able to think about since yesterday.

They stared at each other for several electrified seconds before he moved back slowly, taking his sweet time about it.

"I could have just handed the pen to you," Tamara grumbled, her voice husky with arousal.

His lips twitched. "I didn't want to interrupt your conversation."

"Yeah, right." She looked down at his lab coat. "You have spare pens in your pocket."

He followed the direction of her accusing gaze. "Oops," he murmured. "My bad."

Tamara scowled at him.

When she returned her attention to Sheryl, she found the other woman watching them closely, her eyes glinting with shrewd speculation.

Tamara panicked. "If you two will excuse me," she mumbled, scooping her patient charts off the counter, "I have rounds to make."

And with that, she strode quickly away.

Chapter 7

As she neared the entrance to Bethany Dennison's room two hours later, Tamara heard girlish peals of laughter. Curiosity piqued, she quickened her pace until she reached the open doorway.

She stopped short at the sight that greeted her.

Victor and a small boy, no more than six years old, faced off across the portable overbed table, each gripping the other's hand. Victor was squatting on his haunches, eyes narrowed, face screwed up in a comical expression of concentration.

Bethany sat propped up in bed, her dark hair pulled back from her face in a thick rope of a braid that hung over one shoulder. Tamara was pleased to see how well the lacerations and contusions on her face and arms were healing. And judging by the sound of her laughter, she wasn't experiencing any respiratory problems, which was always a risk for patients who'd undergone a thoracotomy.

Grinning at Victor and her little brother, Bethany asked, "Are you guys ready?"

The boy eagerly bobbed his head.

"Let's do this," Victor said in the low, guttural rasp perfected by Hollywood action heroes.

Bethany's grin widened. "Okay. On the count of three. One…two…three!"

The boy scrunched up his small face, pushing at Victor's arm with all his might. Even from across the room, Tamara could see that Victor wasn't exerting the slightest bit of force, though he did a pretty good job of pretending to.

After several prolonged moments, he surrendered with a loud, exaggerated groan of disappointment.

The boy's eyes widened—first with shock, then with triumphant elation—as he stared at his sister. "I beat him! I beat him!"

Bethany clapped and cheered. "Yay, Decker! Good job!"

Affecting an appropriately humble expression, Victor shook his young opponent's hand. "Congratulations, my man. I shouldn't have doubted you."

Beaming with vindicated delight, Decker Dennison flexed his nonexistent biceps. "Told you I'm strong!"

Victor laughed, playfully ruffling the boy's dark, curly locks. "Guess I need to get out of this hospital more often and start hitting the gym, huh?"

"Yeah, probably," Decker agreed.

Tamara covered her mouth, but her laughter escaped anyway, drawing the attention of the three occupants of the room.

She was amused by the varying reactions to her appearance. Decker waved at her, then plopped into a chair to resume playing his Nintendo DS. While Victor's expression grew shuttered, Bethany's face brightened even more, if that were possible.

"Hi, Dr. St. John!"

"Hello, Bethany," Tamara said, smiling warmly as she advanced into the room. "How are you feeling today?"

Bethany grimaced. "My ribs are still sore, but Dr. Aguilar says that's normal after a thora…thoracot—" She broke off, grinning sheepishly. "How do you pronounce that word again?"

"Tho-ra-cot-o-my," Tamara enunciated. "And Dr. Aguilar is right. Sore ribs are perfectly normal."

"What'd I tell you, kiddo?" Victor drawled humorously. "And she *never* thinks I'm right."

Bethany giggled.

As Tamara reached the bed, Victor moved aside so that she could stand near their patient. "Where's your mom?" she asked Bethany, thinking of the anxious woman who'd been a constant fixture at her daughter's bedside since the accident.

"She went downstairs to meet my father," Bethany replied. "He just got off from work."

Tamara nodded, smiling as she gently passed a hand over the teenager's smooth, wavy hair. "You're looking better and better every day. And the sound of your laughter was music to my ears."

"That's what Dr. Aguilar said." Bethany grinned at them. "You guys think alike."

Tamara and Victor exchanged glances.

"Every now and then," Tamara conceded before her

gaze wandered to the growing assortment of balloons, flowers and teddy bears that had been brought to Bethany during the week.

She smiled. "I do believe you're the most popular patient on this floor, Miss Bethany."

"Yeah." The girl smiled shyly. "A lot of kids and teachers from school came to see me. Even the principal showed up one day."

"That's wonderful," Tamara said warmly. "Isn't it great to know how much you're loved?"

Bethany nodded. "I didn't even know some of the people who visited me." She hesitated, then admitted almost wistfully, "I'm not, like, one of the most popular kids at school. Not even close."

Tamara was touched by the glimpse of vulnerability Bethany had revealed. Suddenly she was reminded of the shy, reclusive nerd *she'd* once been, misunderstood by her peers who hadn't shared her consuming ambition.

"As you're about to discover, kiddo," Victor drawled wryly, "popularity is overrated."

Bethany stared up at him. "You think I'm going to be popular now?"

"You already are. You were the most seriously injured kid on that bus. You were this close—" he held his thumb and forefinger an inch apart "—to doing the tango with the Grim Reaper. Your name's been all over the news, and reporters have been chomping at the bit to talk to you." He flashed a crooked grin. "Helluva way to get famous, isn't it?"

"Tell me about it." A slow, impish smile swept across Bethany's face. "But I'll take it."

"Good Lord," Tamara muttered as Victor threw back his head and roared with laughter.

A few minutes later they were joined by Bethany's parents, an attractive interracial couple in their late thirties. Although Victor and Eli Dennison had already established a rapport, bonding over their love for all things baseball, the man still seemed somewhat uncomfortable around Tamara. She suspected that he, like many brothers who married outside their race, expected to be harshly judged by every black woman he encountered. But he needn't have feared Tamara's condemnation. Although she fully expected to marry a black man someday, she'd never begrudged others for making different choices.

After perching on the side of the bed to hug and kiss his daughter, Eli Dennison looked up at Victor and Tamara with a worried expression. "I know you're sending her home tomorrow, but is she going to be okay? I mean, long-term?"

Tamara was surprised when Victor glanced at her, silently prompting her to respond to the concerned father.

She hesitated, then gently explained, "Bethany's going to experience some pain and discomfort for a while. And you all need to keep a close eye on her incision to make sure there's no redness or swelling, which could mean it's infected. To answer your question regarding her long-term prognosis, I can tell you that the worst part is over. Bethany survived a complicated medical procedure that many don't. She's young, healthy and strong, and incredibly resilient." Tamara smiled. "So something tells me, Mr. Dennison, that your daughter's going to be around for a very long time to drive you crazy over boys, college applications and expensive wedding preparations."

Tears filled the man's dark eyes. "Thank you," he said in a soft, choked voice. "Thanks to both of you for saving our baby girl's life."

Tamara's throat tightened. She could only nod as Chloe Dennison caught and squeezed her husband's hand.

Victor walked over to their son and crouched down, bringing himself to eye level with the boy. "I want you to take good care of your sister, all right? Bring her all the ice cream she wants, and if you see that she's in a lot of pain, let one of your parents know. Can you do that for me, buddy?"

Decker nodded vigorously. "Yes, sir."

Victor grinned, tousling his hair. "Attaboy."

After hugging Bethany and promising to return the next day to go over her discharge instructions, Tamara and Victor left the room.

A companionable silence lapsed between them as they started down the corridor, hands clasped behind their backs, steps perfectly synchronized.

"You have an amazing bedside manner," Tamara blurted, voicing her thoughts aloud without intending to.

"So do you," Victor said at once.

They stopped walking and turned to face each other, their words tumbling over one another's.

"I loved the way you stroked Bethany's hair, giving her that human touch."

"And what about you? Arm wrestling with her little brother like that? It was the most adorable thing I've ever seen."

Victor shook his head. "He's a great kid who loves his sister. The whole family would have fallen apart if anything had happened to her. But that's why I wanted you to answer Mr. Dennison's question. I knew you'd have just the right words to reassure him."

"I really appreciated that," Tamara said earnestly. "But you would have been just as comforting. You really connected with them."

"So did you. I think—" The rest of Victor's sentence was drowned out by the noisy rattle of a passing dinner cart.

He and Tamara smiled sheepishly at each other.

"Talk about a mutual admiration society," she teased.

Victor chuckled softly. "Yeah."

As the humorous moment passed, they stared at each other. Tamara nervously tucked her hands into the pockets of her lab coat. "Well, I'd better—" She broke off at the sound of approaching voices.

Glancing around, she saw two young, attractive nurses strolling toward them. As the women drew near, they smiled so suggestively at Victor that Tamara would have sworn the three of them had just engaged in a *ménage à trois.* Which they probably had at some point.

"Hey, Victor," they cooed. Not Dr. Aguilar. *Victor.*

He inclined his head in greeting. "Ladies."

They continued past, giggling breathlessly like schoolgirls.

Rubbing his jaw as if he were suddenly uncomfortable, Victor reclaimed Tamara's gaze. "Where were we?"

"*I* was about to finish my rounds," she said tightly. "So you're more than welcome to catch up with your little…friends."

He frowned. "What's that supposed to mean?"

She smiled sweetly. "You're the one with the genius IQ. So I'll let you figure it out."

As she stalked off down the hallway, he came after her. "Wait a minute. Can we talk?"

"We just were. Now it's time to get back to work."

"Not yet. We weren't finished."

"Yes, we—"

Without warning, Victor grabbed her arm and tugged her across the corridor to a supply closet. He nudged her inside, then shoved the door closed behind them.

Tamara staggered backward, glaring incredulously at him. "What do you think you're doing? I don't appreciate being manhandled!"

"You didn't leave me any other choice," Victor growled.

She glanced disdainfully around the narrow closet filled with shelves of medical supplies and equipment. "Please don't tell me this is where you have all your quickies."

He scowled. "What the hell are you talking about? What quickies?"

She snorted. "Like you don't know. I've heard—"

"Whatever," he cut her off impatiently. "I just wanted to have a private conversation with you for once. I swear, it feels like we're constantly under a damn microscope around here."

Tamara couldn't argue with that. "Fine," she relented in nervous exasperation. "What do you want to talk about?"

"Us."

Her heart lodged in her throat. Staring at him, she asked warily, "What about us?"

"There's something happening between us, Tamara."

She swallowed hard, fighting panic. "I don't know what you're—"

"Deny it all you want," he said, dangerously soft, "but I know I'm not the only one who sensed a change in our relationship the other night. We made a connection, Tamara. A powerful connection."

She shivered. "Just because we're attracted to each other—"

"Uh-uh," he interrupted, slowly advancing on her. "It's more than that, though God knows if we had any more chemistry, we wouldn't be able to keep our clothes on. No, *cariño,* what we're dealing with here goes way beyond sexual attraction, and I think you know it."

She trembled, her lungs locking as he stopped just inches from her. It was criminal what he did to her, wreaking pure havoc on her body without even laying a finger on her.

"Go out with me, Tamara," he said, low and husky.

She shook her head vehemently. "I can't."

"You can't?" he challenged. "Or you won't?"

"What difference does it make?"

"One implies an inability. The other is a refusal." His eyes glittered. "So which is it?"

"Both," she said in a shaky voice. "You know the policy—"

"Screw the policy," he growled. "The policy didn't stop Jaclyn and Dr. De Winter from getting together."

"And look what it cost them!" Tamara interjected. "Dr. De Winter had to step down as chief resident."

"Yeah, but he's in charge of the E.R. now, so I'd say

things worked out just fine for him. Anyway, we're not talking about anyone else. We're talking about us."

"There is no us," Tamara said emphatically. "I'm sorry, Victor, but I've worked too damn hard to get where I am to allow myself to be sidetracked."

"I'm not trying to sidetrack you. We share the same career goals, remember?"

"Exactly! So you have as much to lose as I do."

"One date, Tamara," Victor cajoled huskily. "All I'm asking for is *one* date."

She wavered, undeniably tempted to surrender, to allow herself to enjoy his company—free of prying eyes—for just one night. But she knew that one date would lead to another, then another. And before she knew it, she'd be in over her head, wondering how she could have been so foolish.

Steeling her resolve, she shook her head firmly. "No, Victor. I can't go out with you. I *won't*. So please just—" She broke off as he tucked his stethoscope into his ears and gently placed the disk on her chest. Her heart galloped as she watched him close his eyes, the dark crescents of his lashes fanning his cheekbones.

After several agonizing moments, she swiped her tongue nervously over her dry lips. "Wh-what are you doing?"

"Listening to your heart." His eyes opened, tunneling deep into hers. "You should try it sometime."

And with those profoundly nuanced words hanging between them, he turned and walked out on her.

Chapter 8

"So who'd you have to sleep with to get an entire day off?" Alejandro Aguilar García teased his older brother the next afternoon.

"Very funny," Victor retorted. "I didn't have to sleep with anyone. And I'm on call, so I could get paged anytime."

Alejandro *tsk-tsked*. "You'll break Mama's heart if you leave early. All she's looked forward to is having you home today. She killed the fatted calf and everything."

Victor chuckled. "Believe me, I'm not going anywhere until I've stuffed my face. My mouth's been watering since I got here and smelled her cooking."

Alejandro grinned. "That's why I have to marry a Colombian woman with some culinary chops. I wouldn't be able to survive without empanadas and *sancocho.*"

"You don't know what you'd be able to survive without," Victor murmured, his mood darkening at the thought of Tamara and the way she'd turned him down yesterday. If she thought he was giving up that easily, she'd better think again.

"Anyway," he added to his brother, "you're too young to be thinking about marriage. You're only a junior in college. Speaking of which, how are your classes going?"

"So far, so good."

Alejandro was an engineering major at Virginia Commonwealth University. To save money, he commuted from their parents' house in Richmond. He didn't mind living at home since he no longer had to share a bedroom with Victor. And he never had to worry about cooking or washing his own laundry, because his mother did everything for him. With his dark hair, swarthy complexion, blue eyes and the killer grin he unleashed at will, Alejandro would undoubtedly have no trouble finding another woman to cater to his needs when he finally left the nest.

The Aguilars' modest brick house rested on three acres of land, a good portion of which had been converted into a scaled-down backyard baseball field. Sprawled on old lawn chairs, Victor and Alejandro watched from the sidelines as their younger brothers and cousins, along with some neighborhood friends, competed in a spirited baseball game.

Their youngest brother, Roberto, was now at bat. The fourteen-year-old made a show of adjusting his cap over his blue eyes, scuffing at the dirt and spitting through his teeth in his best imitation of his idol, Colombian-born shortstop Edgar Rentería. The opposing players, waiting in the outfield, scoffed at Roberto's antics and rolled their eyes at one another.

But their taunts were silenced moments later when Roberto swung his bat, which connected with the ball with a sharp crack. As the baseball went sailing across the azure sky, the boy grinned and sprinted toward first base.

Cupping his hands around his mouth, Victor called out encouragingly, *"Vamos, Roberto, corre rápido!"*

As Roberto rounded the bases and crossed home plate, Victor and Alejandro stood and cheered, then high-fived each other before returning to their seats.

"That kid's gonna be something special," Victor proudly declared. "He's got raw talent."

"Hell, yeah," Alejandro agreed. "I can't wait to see him in the big leagues one day."

They watched as Roberto's home run was boister-ously celebrated by his teammates, which included their other brothers Christian and Fernando, along with Luis Aguilar, who'd been coaching his sons' baseball teams since they were young.

Normally, Victor and Alejandro also participated in the game. But today both had chosen the role of spec-tator, content to enjoy the warm fall weather as they watched the competitive exhibition.

Lazily stretching out his long legs, Alejandro slanted Victor an amused sidelong glance. "So how are things going at Hopewell General? Or should I just call it Gen-eral Hospital, since that place has more drama than a damn soap opera?"

Victor chuckled, taking a long pull on his beer.

"Things are going as well as can be expected under the circumstances."

"You think that guy is gonna win the lawsuit?"

"If he doesn't," Victor said sardonically, "it won't be for lack of trying on his family's part."

"I know," Alejandro agreed with a grimace. "They're really pulling out the knives, aren't they? I heard they recently did an interview where they questioned the chief of staff's management skills and cited some unnamed source who claims the guy is a womanizer. Is that true?"

Victor kept his expression neutral. "No comment."

Alejandro laughed. "Who can blame the man? You work with some fine-ass women, *hermanote.* Remember that time I met you for lunch and you introduced me to a couple of your fellow interns? I don't remember their names, but damn." He sketched an hourglass with his hands, then kissed his fingertips. *"Muy bonita!"*

Victor chuckled dryly. "Their names are Isabelle and Jaclyn. And, yes, they're both very beautiful."

"Even the one you didn't introduce me to—the one you don't like. Man, she's a hottie, too." Alejandro grinned wickedly, shaking his head. "I don't know how you keep your hands to yourself."

If only you knew, Victor mused darkly.

"So how's she doing, anyway? The sexy chocolate one. What was her name again?"

"Tamara."

"Yeah, Tamara," Alejandro said, snapping his fingers. "How's she doing? You still beefing with her?"

"Something like that," Victor mumbled, taking a swig of his beer.

Alejandro's blue eyes glinted wickedly. "You should sleep with her."

Victor choked on his drink. As he coughed and gasped, his brother reached over and pounded him on the back.

Scowling, Victor wiped his mouth with the back of his hand and demanded hoarsely, "What the hell did you just say?"

Alejandro grinned. "You heard me. I think you should sleep with Tamara. Can you imagine how hot the sex would be? It'd be like makeup sex—all that anger and aggression and…*¡Dios Mio!* I need to find myself a Tamara."

Victor shook his head in disgust. *"Culo."*

His brother laughed. "Why do I have to be an ass just because I'm suggesting what you know you secretly want to do?"

When Victor didn't deny it, Alejandro laughed even harder. "I knew it! When I asked you over lunch that day why you didn't introduce me to Tamara, you spent the next twenty minutes griping about some argument you'd just had with her, telling me what a stubborn smart-ass she was. I'd never seen you so worked up over a woman. The more you bitched about her, the more I realized you were seriously lusting after her."

"Vete al carajo," Victor grumbled rancorously.

Alejandro laughed again. "So when are you gonna bring her home to meet the family?"

Victor frowned. "How did we go from me wanting to sleep with her," he growled, "to introducing her to my family?"

"I was just joking." Alejandro grinned ruefully. "You

know how Mama and Papa are. They wouldn't take too kindly to you bringing a sister home."

"I know," Victor muttered grimly.

"It's a shame," Alejandro lamented with a shake of his head. "Sometimes they act like we didn't grow up around any Afro-Colombians. Like Afro-Colombians didn't have a hand in securing Colombian independence. I bet even *you* didn't know that the hero of the Battle of Pantano de Vargas, Juan José Rondón, was the son of African slaves."

"Actually, I did know that." Victor gave his brother an amused look. "But when did you become such a history buff?"

"I'm not," Alejandro admitted sheepishly. "This girl at school had to educate me. She's a history major, and smart as hell. One night we were studying for an exam and got to talking about our families. I told her how my parents aren't racist, but they'd have a problem with any of us marrying a black woman. Amani—that's her name—got a little offended. And that's when she started schooling me about the historical contributions of black Colombians."

Victor chuckled. "Good for her."

"I know. I've never felt so dumb in my life."

"You're not dumb. You just need to broaden your horizons."

"That's what Amani said."

"Smart woman." Victor grinned slyly. "Is she pretty?"

"Very." Alejandro's smile bordered on dreamy. "You know that saying, 'The blacker the berry, the sweeter the juice'?"

Victor nodded.

"That's Amani all the way. Fine as hell."

"Uh-oh." Victor gave his brother a knowing grin. "Sounds to me like someone's got himself a serious crush."

"No, I don't," Alejandro mumbled, even as a bright flush crept over his face. "We're just study partners."

"Study partners, huh?"

"Yeah, man. Like I said, she's really smart and—hey!" he laughingly protested as Victor reached over and grabbed him, putting him in a headlock the way he'd done when they were children.

"Jandro has a crush," he chanted teasingly as his brother tried to squirm out of his playful grasp.

"A crush on who?"

Victor and Alejandro looked up to find their mother standing there, her eyes filled with unabashed curiosity.

As they rose to their feet, Alejandro said quickly, "No one, Mama."

"No one?" Marcela Aguilar divided a speculative glance between her two sons. "Then why is your brother teasing you?"

"You know how Victor is. He's always teasing me about something. Is it time to eat?" Alejandro asked abruptly.

"Yes. Your *tía* and the girls will be bringing the food outside—"

"I'll help them," Alejandro offered, and strode off toward the house.

His mother stared after him for a moment, then turned back to Victor, her delicate brows inquisitively raised. "What's wrong with your brother?"

Victor grinned. "Nothing, Mama," he said, gently

folding her into his arms and kissing her forehead. "Absolutely nothing."

Marcela Aguilar was a petite firebrand of a woman with expressive brown eyes, milky-smooth skin and dark, lustrous hair that hung nearly to her small waist.

She angled her head back to peer into Victor's face, an affectionate smile curving her mouth. "I'm so glad you're here, *mijo*. I was afraid the hospital would call you to go to work."

"They still might," Victor reluctantly admitted.

"They won't. And if they do," she added with a conspiratorial wink, "you won't answer the phone."

Victor chuckled, and refrained from telling her that he was already treading on thin ice at the hospital. The last thing he wanted was to make her worry.

As her soft hand tenderly cradled his cheek, she clucked her tongue. "When are you going to shave? Are you trying to grow a beard?"

"No, Mama. I just haven't given shaving much thought."

"You're working too hard," she fretted. "When do you have time for a social life?"

"I don't. But that's not a priority right now. Getting through my residency is what's important."

"But—"

He groaned in soft exasperation. "Mama, stop worrying about me. You're giving yourself gray hairs."

She looked stricken. "Where?" she asked, self-consciously patting her head.

Victor grinned. "Nowhere. I just wanted to distract you. Now let's go eat. I'm starving."

"Good. I made your favorites."

"Bandeja Paisa? Arroz con coco?"

She smiled indulgently. "Of course, *papito.*"

He kissed both of her cheeks with an exuberance that made her laugh.

"Help me gather everyone for lunch," she told him, "and then we can eat."

As they started across the sprawling backyard, his arm around her shoulders and hers around his waist, Marcela sighed deeply.

Victor glanced at her. "What is it?"

"I want you to be happy, Victor. Being a doctor is important, but so is your happiness."

"Why do they have to be mutually exclusive? Why can't I be a doctor *and* be happy?"

"You can, of course." She stared off pensively toward the baseball field where the players were ending their game, the winners celebrating with hearty back slaps and high fives.

"I know things didn't work out with Natalia," Marcela gently continued. "As much as I liked her, I can see why she might not have been right for you. But if you meet someone else—someone you think could be special—I want you to bring her home. Let us get to know her."

Victor was silent, his thoughts inexorably returning to Tamara.

"Mijo?" his mother prompted after several moments, eyeing him hopefully. "Will you do that? Will you let us meet her?"

"Maybe I will," he said quietly. "Maybe I will."

Chapter 9

For the second time in less than a week, Tamara found herself entering the inner sanctum of Dr. Germaine Dudley's office. After receiving some troubling news from Dr. Balmer, Tamara had asked Jaclyn to cover for her, then had hurried upstairs to the floor that housed the hospital's administrative offices.

She was trying to set up an appointment through Dr. Dudley's assistant, Mona Wells, when the chief of staff poked his head out the door to bark out a question to the woman. When he saw Tamara standing there, he frowned.

"Do we have a meeting scheduled, Dr. St. John? Because I don't remember seeing anything on my calendar."

"Um, no, sir. We don't. But I was hoping to speak to you, if you have a few minutes?"

He hesitated, eyeing her suspiciously.

"Please, Dr. Dudley?" she implored. "It's very important."

He wavered for another moment, then relented with a curt nod.

Tamara followed him into the office and closed the door, but not before she caught a glimpse of his assistant eagerly reaching for her desk phone, no doubt to call one of her cronies to speculate about the reason for Tamara's visit.

Grimacing at the thought, Tamara walked over to the visitor's chair she'd occupied last Friday. She didn't miss the way Dr. Dudley's eyes traveled over her, lingering on her breasts long enough to make her skin crawl, but not long enough to be accused of openly leering.

With his dark skin, broad forehead and keen dark eyes, the sixty-something chief of staff was almost a dead ringer for Danny Glover. He was also married and the father of three, which meant he should know better than to subject his female subordinates to his lecherous tendencies.

As Tamara sat down across from the man's large desk, she said, "Thank you for agreeing to see me."

"If you're here to make another appeal for the research grant—"

"Actually, sir," she interrupted, "I'm here to talk to you about Dr. Aguilar."

Dudley's expression darkened with displeasure. "What about him?"

Tamara hesitated, swallowing nervously. She knew she was taking a huge risk by coming here like this, but after what she'd just learned, she'd felt that she had to do something.

Dudley made an impatient sound. "I don't have all day, Dr. St. John."

"Sorry." She took a deep breath, willing her stomach to stop churning with nerves. "Dr. Balmer informed me that you might be taking disciplinary action against Dr. Aguilar. So I came to ask you to reconsider."

The chief stared at her as if she'd taken complete leave of her senses, which she probably had. "I beg your pardon?"

Refusing to be cowed by his imperious tone, Tamara bravely forged ahead. "I don't know what sort of disciplinary measures you're considering, but I think it would be a mistake to kick Dr. Aguilar out of the residency program."

"Is that so?" Dudley's tone was faintly mocking. "*You* think it would be a mistake?"

"Yes, sir, I do. Dr. Aguilar is a gifted doctor, one of the best—if not *the* best—in our group. And I say that as someone who doesn't always agree with his approach to medicine."

"Based on what I've heard," Dudley interjected, "you never agree."

"Well, let's just say we often agree to disagree," Tamara countered diplomatically. "But whatever differences I may have with Dr. Aguilar doesn't change what I just said about him." She paused. "Are you familiar with the saying 'Iron sharpens iron'?"

He frowned. "Of course."

"Well, that's how I feel about most of my fellow interns. We encourage and support one another, but more than that, we sharpen one another. Dr. Aguilar makes me a better doctor. So not having him around would be…well, it would be a tremendous loss."

Dr. Dudley leaned back slowly in his chair, his hands steepled in front of his chest, his eyes narrowed on her face in shrewd speculation.

"I'm not condoning the way he spoke to you," Tamara hastened to continue. "I think he was out of line, and I told him so. But I understand where he was coming from. He was disappointed and frustrated—"

"So were you," Dudley interrupted tersely, "yet *you* managed to keep your emotions, and your tongue, in check. What's Dr. Aguilar's excuse?"

"Maybe it's that passionate Latin blood running through his veins?" Tamara offered meekly, spreading her hands as if to say, *What can you do?*

Dudley was not amused. "Let me make sure I understand you correctly, Dr. St. John. Are you asking me to tolerate Dr. Aguilar's insubordination because—what? You'll miss him if he's gone?"

Heat rushed to her face. "No, of course not. And I'm not asking you to 'tolerate' anything. I'm just asking you to give him a second chance. He's passionate about his work, whether he's treating patients or lobbying for more money to advance his medical research. He genuinely cares about people, and it shows in everything he does. He belongs here."

"With all due respect, young lady," Dudley said curtly, "*I'll* determine whether or not Dr. Aguilar belongs at Hopewell General."

Tamara held his stern gaze for a long moment, then said with quiet conviction, "Whether he's here or somewhere else, Dr. Aguilar *is* going to be a brilliant cardiothoracic surgeon. If I were in your position, sir, I'd want him here, playing for my team."

Dudley glared at her. "Are you finished?"

"I suppose I am." Slowly she rose from her chair. "Thank you for your time."

The chief said nothing.

She had reached the door when his voice stopped her. "Dr. St. John?"

She turned to look at him.

"You should know that I had already made a decision regarding Dr. Aguilar's future," he said levelly. "But now, in view of this *enlightening* conversation we've had…well, let's just say you've given me even more food for thought."

Tamara swallowed hard, searching his face for some clue that would give her insight into the decision he'd reached. But his impenetrable expression betrayed nothing, much to her chagrin.

Had she helped Victor's case? she wondered. Or had she made things worse for him?

Dismayed at the thought, she turned and walked out of Dr. Dudley's office.

Later that evening, Tamara, Jaclyn and Isabelle were having coffee in the break room. One moment they were discussing the vagaries of HMOs, which they'd already grown to detest as doctors. No sooner had that conversation ended than Isabelle turned to Tamara and blurted, "So why'd you turn Victor down when he asked you out?"

Tamara nearly spat out her coffee. Sputtering and dabbing at her mouth with a napkin, she stared at Isabelle. "Who told you that?"

"He did."

"*He* told you?" Tamara was stunned. "Why?"

Isabelle chuckled wryly. "Yesterday I was teasing

him about the hospital needing to take out an insurance policy on the two of you, because one of these days, you're likely to start throwing chairs at each other during one of your famous arguments."

"Like the one we overheard when you were on the elevator last week," Jaclyn added.

Tamara's face heated at the memory of how that particular argument had ended.

"Anyway," Isabelle continued, "I told Victor that you two seemed to be bickering more frequently lately, and he admitted that he didn't want to be at war with you anymore. That's when he told me that he'd asked you out on a date, but you shot him down."

Tamara shook her head, torn between incredulity and annoyance. "I can't believe he told you about that."

Isabelle looked baffled. "Why?"

"What do you mean? Because you two used to date."

"We did?"

"Of course. Everyone knows that." Tamara looked askance at Jaclyn. "Didn't they?"

Jaclyn shook her head, hazel eyes twinkling. "They never dated."

"What?" Tamara's surprised gaze swung back to Isabelle. "But I thought—"

"You thought wrong, girlfriend." Isabelle grinned. "Victor and I are just friends, and that's all we've ever been."

Tamara frowned. "But I distinctly remember a night, months ago, when you left the hospital together because you had a date."

"It wasn't a date. I treated him to dinner because he'd helped me move into Jaclyn's condo. It was purely platonic."

Once again, Tamara looked to their fellow intern for confirmation.

Jaclyn smiled. "It's true."

"Wow," Tamara said, meeting Isabelle's amused gaze. "And all this time I thought the two of you had a thing."

"Nope. Now don't get me wrong," Isabelle added. "I think Victor is sexy as hell, and any woman would be lucky to have him—"

Tamara snorted. "I think most members of the nursing staff *have* had him."

Isabelle and Jaclyn exchanged quick glances. "Wrong again."

"Come on," Tamara scoffed. "Do you guys really expect me to believe that Victor hasn't gotten around? I've heard the rumors, and I've seen the way some of these nurses look at him, like he's a juicy piece of meat they've already sampled and want more of."

Isabelle and Jaclyn laughed.

"They might *wish* they've sampled him—" Jaclyn said.

"—but none of them have," Isabelle finished.

Tamara eyed the two women skeptically. "What are you saying? That Victor *doesn't* have a harem of naughty nurses?"

"Only in their dreams," Isabelle said with a snort. "They think Victor's a hottie, which is why they nicknamed him 'Dr. *Caliente.*' And most of them would jump at the chance to sleep with him, especially the ones who've actually come out and propositioned him."

"Girl, you can't imagine how bold and scandalous some of these chicks are," Jaclyn added.

"Oh, I can imagine," Tamara muttered, remembering Victor's discomfiture when they'd encountered the two young nurses in the hallway on Saturday.

Isabelle continued, "He's been cornered in X-ray rooms and supply closets. And he's found everything from phone numbers to edible condoms in the pockets of his lab coat. The rumors you've heard were probably started by some of the very same women who've been trying to seduce him. But Victor has never slept with any of them."

Tamara frowned. "How do you and Jaclyn know all this?"

Isabelle chuckled. "Ravi gave us the lowdown. He and Victor are really good friends, so sometimes after work they go out for beers and swap stories about the stalker du jour. Don't forget that most of these women throw themselves at Ravi, too, even though he's engaged." She shook her head. "If the situation were reversed, these same females would consider themselves the victims of sexual harassment. But the fellas get a pretty good laugh over everything."

Tamara sipped her lukewarm coffee, pondering the implications of what she'd just learned. Was it possible that she'd misjudged Victor? Was it possible that he *wasn't* a charming womanizer looking to add her to his stable of conquests?

Watching her face, Isabelle grinned knowingly. "You have the look of someone who's experiencing a major paradigm shift."

"Hmm," Tamara murmured noncommittally.

"Now, obviously, I can't speak for what Victor does outside the hospital. But I can tell you that when he's here, his mind is on work. That is, as long as *you're* not around," Isabelle added slyly. "When you're around, there's no telling where his mind goes."

"I know that's right," Jaclyn concurred, grinning at Tamara. "It's pretty obvious that you and Victor drive each other to distraction."

"But we still get our work done," Tamara said almost defensively. "We've never allowed our personal, er, issues to interfere with our treatment of patients."

"No one's saying you have," Jaclyn assured her. "In fact, you both work so well together that everyone has noticed."

"Which is why you should go out with him," Isabelle suggested. "Beneath the cocky exterior, Victor's a really sweet guy. I mean, he talks to his mother on the phone every day. Once when she was sick, I overheard him singing a Colombian lullaby to her."

"Aww," Jaclyn sighed, laying a hand over her heart. "That is *so* sweet."

Tamara had to agree. Being a mama's girl herself, she'd always been a sucker for a man with a soft spot for his mother.

"So give him a chance, Tamara," Isabelle urged. "At least let him take you out to dinner."

Tamara shrugged. "I might consider it," she said, feigning nonchalance. "But I don't think he'll ask me out again."

Isabelle smiled. "I wouldn't be too sure about that. If he likes you as much as we suspect he does, you haven't heard the last of him."

Suddenly that didn't sound like such a bad thing, Tamara thought.

Wanting to change the subject, she glanced at Jaclyn, who was toying with the plastic lid on her coffee cup.

"Are you okay?" Tamara asked her.

Jaclyn glanced up, meeting her concerned gaze. "I'm fine."

"You don't look fine. You seem preoccupied."

Jaclyn hesitated, then sighed. "I guess I'm just worried about me and Lucien. Now that we're engaged, it seems as if Dr. Dudley's got it in for us more than ever."

Tamara nodded sympathetically. Although Jaclyn and Lucien De Winter were undeniably meant for each other, their relationship remained under intense scrutiny. But now, in light of some news Tamara had received earlier, Dr. Dudley's fixation on the couple seemed downright hypocritical.

"I know something that should make you feel better about your engagement to Dr. De Winter," Tamara said.

Jaclyn stared alertly at her. "What?"

Grinning mischievously, Tamara propped her elbows on the table and leaned toward her two companions. "I was talking to Jerome a few hours ago," she confided in a low voice, "and he told me the most scandalous secret he's been keeping for days."

"What secret?" Jaclyn and Isabelle breathed.

"Well, it seems that Jerome caught Dr. Dudley and Nurse Tsang having sex in a supply closet."

"Get out of here!" Jaclyn and Isabelle shrieked, gaping at her incredulously. "Are you serious?"

"As a heart attack." Tamara winced, thinking of her chosen specialty. "No pun intended."

The two women burst out laughing.

"The nerve of those two!" Jaclyn exclaimed indignantly. "They're always harassing others about adhering to the nonfraternization policy, yet there *they* are, screwing in a supply closet!"

"I wish I knew which one it was," Isabelle chortled. "I'd never step foot inside it again. Can you imagine Dudley and Tsang doing the nasty?"

The three women looked at each other, then let out a collective, *"Eeeuuuwww!"*

Chapter 10

Throughout the next day, Tamara remained in a heightened state of awareness, thanks to Victor. Every time he came near her, her pulse hammered erratically, and her skin felt singed. She could feel the heat of his eyes on her whenever she walked into a room. During the interns' weekly group briefing with Dr. Balmer, Tamara didn't hear a word that was spoken. The intensity of Victor's gaze scrambled her circuits, rendering her unable to concentrate. But when she glanced over her shoulder, he was staring toward the front of the room, listening to their supervisor with a look of focused absorption.

At the end of the long, nerve-racking day, she emerged from the hospital to find Victor sitting astride a gleaming black and silver motorcycle. His eyes were shaded by mirrored sunglasses, and his long legs were covered in dark Levi's that stretched taut across his strong, muscular thighs.

Her mouth ran dry. "Victor."

"Hey, beautiful," he murmured. "Want a ride?"

She wanted a ride all right, but not necessarily the kind he was offering. She'd thought he couldn't look any sexier than he did in his scrubs, but damn, was she wrong. He looked hot as *hell* on his Harley, straddling the powerful bike with an innate, dangerous-edged masculinity that sent her hormones into overdrive. She wanted to hop on to the seat with him, thrust her breasts into his face and wrap her legs around his back.

Slowly, he removed his sunglasses and tucked them into the front pocket of his battered leather jacket. Her heart thudded as those mesmerizing blue eyes locked with hers.

"Let me give you a ride home."

She swallowed hard, shaking her head. "That's okay. I can walk."

"Why walk," he drawled, "when you can ride?"

Her bones turned to gelatin. "I only live fifteen minutes away."

"I'll get you there in five."

She glanced pointedly at the black helmet dangling from the motorcycle's handlebars. "You don't have one of those for me."

"Actually," he said, reaching inside a compartment next to the gas tank and producing another helmet, "I do." He held her gaze. "So let me take you home."

Tamara wavered, biting her lower lip.

"Get on, *cariño*." His voice dropped an octave, going indecently husky. "You know you want to."

That did it.

Tamara forced herself to walk—not run—over to him. His eyes glinted with wicked satisfaction as he handed the helmet to her, then reached for his own. They stared at each other as they settled the protective gear over their heads.

Get on, Victor mouthed to her.

Pulse racing, Tamara swung her leg over the seat and wrapped her arms around his lean waist.

He glanced over his shoulder at her. "Ready?"

She nodded. "Ready."

He turned the key in the ignition. The monster engine revved to life, vibrating the ground and rumbling through the air like the primal roar of a jungle beast.

Tamara's arms tightened around Victor as he pulled away from the curb and cruised through the parking lot. They left the hospital grounds and hit Route One, which wasn't congested at that late hour. Taking advantage of the open road, Victor went full throttle, roaring down the street with a speed that sent pure adrenaline rushing through Tamara's veins. Although she wasn't surprised that he drove like a demon road warrior, she felt completely safe with him. And as the wind whipped through the ends of her hair, she threw back her head and laughed, feeling more vibrantly alive than she had in years.

Victor took the long way home, weaving through historic Old Town Alexandria with its cobblestone streets, colonial houses, museums, shops and restaurants. They meandered down Prince Street, which ran parallel to the Potomac and offered scenic views of the glistening river that separated Northern Virginia from Washington, D.C. Tamara had lived in Alexandria all her life, but that night she took in the beautiful sights as if she were seeing them for the very first time. She didn't want the ride to end. Snuggled against Victor's body, savoring his heat and masculine strength, she could have stayed right there forever.

All too soon, he pulled up in front of a modern apartment building surrounded by shade trees.

He held the motorcycle upright as Tamara climbed off and removed her helmet. She smiled shyly at him, watching as he lifted his helmet shield to gaze at her. Raising her voice to be heard above the rumbling engine, she told him, "Thanks for the ride—even though it took longer than five minutes."

He smiled lazily. "I said I could get you home in five minutes. I didn't say I actually *would*."

Tamara laughed. "Semantics."

His eyes glinted with amusement.

As she passed him the spare helmet, their fingers brushed. Tingles of awareness shot through her veins, quickening her pulse. "Well, um, thanks again for bringing me home."

"You're welcome."

They stared at each other, neither making a move to leave.

"Would you like to come up for some coffee?" Tamara blurted.

"Absolutely," Victor said.

She directed him to park in one of her reserved spaces, then waited for him to rejoin her. As she watched him saunter toward the building—helmet tucked beneath his arm, dark hair falling rakishly over his forehead—her heart drummed against her ribcage. She knew she was playing with fire by inviting him up to her apartment. But she couldn't have turned him away if her life depended on it. Right or wrong, she wanted to spend more time with him. She'd worry about the consequences later.

When he reached her, she sang teasingly, "B-b-b-bad. Bad to the bone."

Victor grinned. "And don't you forget it," he retorted, playfully swatting her backside.

Laughing, Tamara led him through the small lobby to the bank of elevators. They boarded and claimed opposite corners of the empty car. As they silently gazed at each other, Tamara knew she wasn't the only one remembering the previous elevator ride they'd shared.

They remained silent as they got off and walked to the door of Tamara's apartment. She could feel the heat radiating from Victor's body as he stood close behind her, making her so nervous that she fumbled with the lock three times before getting the door open.

She entered the apartment, flipped a light switch, then gestured Victor inside.

Brushing past her, he glanced around the small living room that featured a slightly worn camelback sofa, a glass coffee table and an oak bookcase crammed with medical tomes.

Setting down his helmet on the console table and peeling off his leather jacket, he remarked, "Nice place."

"Thanks," Tamara said, taking his jacket and hanging it up in the foyer closet. "I'm probably overpaying, but I appreciate living so close to the hospital. I have a car that I rarely drive, because I prefer to walk everywhere."

"How healthy of you," Victor teased, following her as she headed toward the kitchen to start the coffee.

"That, and it's better for the environment." She smiled, glancing over her shoulder at him. "Where do you live?"

"Tidewater Terrace."

"Oh, yeah. I know that place. It was on my list of maybes, but in the end I decided it wasn't close enough to the hospital. Do you like living there?"

"I wouldn't exactly say that," Victor drawled, leaning in the doorway with one shoulder propped on the wall. "It's just a place to lay my head."

Tamara nodded. "I feel the same way about this place. I'm hardly ever home. When I'm not at the hospital, I'm at my mom's house in Maryland."

"Maryland? I thought you grew up in Alexandria."

"I did," Tamara confirmed, rummaging through the cupboard. "After I left home for college, my mother decided she needed a change of scenery, so she moved to Fort Washington."

"I love how close the two of you are," Victor said smilingly. "One of the first times I ever met your mother, she was bringing you lunch just to make sure you didn't starve yourself."

Tamara grinned. "I know. She can't help fussing over me." She paused, brows furrowing. "Oh, shoot."

"What?"

"I'm all out of coffee."

"That's okay. I wasn't really in the mood for coffee, anyway."

"It's just as well. Mine probably wouldn't have met your standards."

"Why?" Victor drawled wryly. "Because I'm Colombian?"

"Exactly," Tamara said with a laugh, walking to the refrigerator and opening the door. After surveying the meager contents, she sighed. "I need to go grocery shopping. All I've got is water and wine. So take your pick."

When Victor didn't respond, she glanced over to catch him with his head tipped to one side, his gaze latched on to her butt. She should have been offended—except she'd been doing the same thing to him almost from the day she met him.

Feeling naughty, she purred coyly, "Like what you see?"

The eyes that traveled back up to her face had a downright wicked gleam. *"Sí,"* Victor said silkily, *"me gusta mucho."*

Tamara's belly quivered. They stared at each other, the air between them crackling with pure sexual electricity.

"Want some wine?" she asked softly.

He held her gaze. "If that's what you're offering."

"It is." Slowly, deliberately, she closed the refrigerator door and faced him. "But that doesn't have to be all."

Their eyes held for one searing moment.

The next thing Tamara knew, Victor was right there, reaching her in two powerful strides and slamming his mouth down on hers. Desire exploded through her body as he parted her lips with his and kissed her with a scorching hunger that stole her breath. She threw her arms around his neck, her hands tangling in the warm, thick silk of his hair.

He lifted her into his arms and, without hesitation, she wrapped her legs around his waist, moaning at the feel of his thick, rigid erection pressing against her crotch. His tongue explored her mouth with deep, sensual strokes that made heat pool between her thighs and seep onto her panties.

They kissed feverishly as he carried her over to the small breakfast table and set her down on the edge. He grasped the hem of her shirt and yanked it over her head, then tossed it aside as Tamara reached behind to unclasp and shrug off her bra. Victor's big hands were already waiting to cup her breasts as they spilled free, the sight of them tearing a hoarse, guttural sound from his throat.

As her nipples hardened beneath his fiercely ravenous gaze, he swore again before his hot mouth latched on to her breast.

Tamara gasped, arching backward on a deep, shuddering moan. His wet tongue caressed her taut nipple with sensuous, velvety strokes she felt deep in her womb. Her hands fisted in his hair, holding him to her as she gave herself over to the exquisite sensations coursing through her body.

As Victor licked and kissed his way to her other breast, his hands went to work on unzipping her jeans. As he began sliding them off, Tamara raised her hips to facilitate the swift removal.

When his fingers gripped the waistband of her panties, their gazes locked.

That was the moment Tamara could have come to her senses and stopped what they were doing, before it was too late.

But she couldn't.

More telling, she didn't want to.

Reading the unmistakable surrender in her eyes, Victor quickly peeled off her panties and set them aside, then knelt between her legs. She trembled with anticipation and need as he lifted her thighs and settled them over his broad, muscular shoulders.

Watching her face intently, he began kissing his way up the inside of her thighs, igniting a path of scorched nerve endings. Anticipation wound inside her, heightening her arousal until she thought she would explode.

"So beautiful," Victor uttered huskily, his smoldering sapphire gaze fastened on the glistening folds of her labia. "So damn beautiful."

Tamara watched, pulse hammering, as he continued working his slow way toward her pulsing core. It was the sweetest, most agonizing torment she'd ever endured—the whisper of his warm breath, the brush of his soft lips, the gentle rasp of his stubble-roughened jaw.

"Victor," she whimpered helplessly, begging him to stop torturing her. "I need…I want—"

The instant his mouth touched her sex, she let out a strangled cry and flung back her head. His tongue stroked the plump folds of her labia, tasting and savoring her. She moaned, her fingers gripping the edges of the table, her toes curling tightly. As he ate at her like she was dripping with honey, she licked her lips and ground her throbbing sex into his face.

When he penetrated her with his tongue, her hips flew off the table as she came with a high-pitched cry. Victor gripped her butt tightly, showing her no mercy as he bit and sucked her clit, bringing her to another shockingly intense orgasm.

When he finally released her, she collapsed weakly onto the table and closed her eyes, waiting for the violent spasms to taper off.

Victor stood and leaned over her, his mouth taking hers in a long, deep, provocative kiss that soon had her aching for more.

"You are one tasty morsel, Dr. St. John," he whispered against her lips.

"Mmm," Tamara purred, sensually rubbing her calves along his strong, denim-covered thighs. "And you, Dr. Aguilar, are one talented man. Who would have guessed?"

He chuckled softly, his hands braced on either side of her head as he gazed down at her, his dark hair falling forward. He was so damn sexy that she got turned on just looking at him.

"So," she murmured throatily, "what other talents do you possess?"

"Mmm," he rumbled, subtly rolling his hips against her. "Depends on what you have in mind."

She cupped the huge bulge tenting the front of his jeans, making him hiss. "*This* is what I have in—"

He was already drawing back from her and tugging off his shirt. Tamara sat up all the way to help him unzip his jeans and slide them down, along with his dark briefs.

Her sex quivered at the sight of his long, thick shaft and powerful male body. She reached up, running her hands down his hard-muscled chest and washboard abs before curling her fingers around his hot, throbbing erection. He groaned as she stroked him, slowly pumping up and down until clear fluid leaked out from the narrow slit. She leaned forward and lapped at the salty-sweet wetness.

Victor jerked, his stomach muscles contracting.

Aroused by his reaction, she wrapped her mouth around his smooth, thick hardness and sucked him down her throat.

"Mierda!" he swore, low and guttural.

A few moments inside her mouth was all he could endure. Pulling out of her, he fisted his hand around his glistening shaft and commanded, "Turn over. I wanna take you from behind."

By the time Tamara got on all fours, the swollen head of his penis was already probing her slick opening. She looked over her shoulder, watching as he slowly, provocatively, stroked his hard length along her cleft. As spasms of pleasure tore through her groin, she moaned and gyrated her hips against him.

As their gazes locked, he entered her with one deep, savage stroke. Tamara cried out sharply and arched her back as Victor groaned—a sound of unadulterated masculine pleasure that sent chills through her, it was so erotic.

She bent over the table and propped herself up on her elbows as he began thrusting into her, one long stroke after the other. She whimpered, the sensations so intensely sublime she thought she'd suffocate.

As his rhythm grew thicker and faster, she tilted her hips back to meet each demanding thrust. He slapped her butt and she cried out, heat stabbing into her loins.

"You like that?" Victor rumbled with satisfaction.

"Sí," she moaned lustily, *"me gusta mucho."*

He laughed, dark and wicked, before smacking her butt again, making her flesh quiver beneath his palm.

She reached behind her to grab his flexing ass, her fingernails digging into the sinewy muscle. He shuddered convulsively, his heavy balls slamming against her bottom. Their coupling was raw and unbearably arousing, like nothing she'd ever experienced before.

"Ah, Tamara," Victor groaned raggedly. "You feel so good, baby. Shit…"

She stared at his face, hard and flushed with passion, his blue eyes glittering fiercely with hunger. She'd never seen anything so powerfully sexy.

He leaned down and slipped his tongue inside her mouth as his fingers simultaneously stroked her erect nipples. Her heart pounded uncontrollably as the tempo of his thrusts increased, sending her breasts bouncing up and down. The kitchen was soon filled with their desperate cries and moans, mingled with the carnal sounds of flesh slapping flesh.

As an explosive pressure built inside Tamara, she mewled breathlessly, "Ohh…I'm coming!"

She sobbed Victor's name, her stomach convulsed in an orgasm that tore through her with such violence, tears ran down her face.

Victor slid halfway out of her, then plunged deep and hard, one last powerful thrust that locked their bodies together. He called her name hoarsely as he came, shuddering so forcefully he rocked the table.

After a few minutes they collapsed on top of it, his sweaty chest heaving against her back as they panted for air.

"Whoa," Tamara breathed when she could speak again, staring at the wall through heavy-lidded eyes. Her vision was so blurred she couldn't tell what color the paint was. "What was *that?*"

Victor shook his head against her. "Words can't even describe it."

They shared a small, breathless laugh.

Sprawled across the table, the wood warm and smooth beneath her naked body, Tamara sighed. "I don't think I'll ever be able to eat on this again."

Victor chuckled. "Then we'll just use it for our purposes."

She glanced over her shoulder at him, her brow arched. "And what makes you think this wasn't a one-time thing?"

"I don't think." He kissed between her shoulder blades, the soft scrape of his bearded jaw making her shiver. "I *know*."

She smiled. "Confident, aren't we?"

"Damn straight." He tugged the scrunchie from her ponytail and combed his fingers through the thick, damp tresses. "I want you to wear your hair down for me sometime."

She raised both brows at the proprietary request. "Confident *and* bossy. Hmm, I don't know about you, man."

"No?" he murmured, his erection thickening against the small of her back. "Then maybe we need to get even better acquainted."

"Mmm," Tamara purred, provocatively rubbing against him, "maybe."

Without further ado, Victor gathered her into his arms, lifted her off the table and carried her down the hall to her bedroom, where they commenced round two.

An hour later, they lay spent in each other's arms, Victor's shaft nestled between their bodies, his hand lazily caressing the curve of her spine.

Tamara sighed languorously. She'd never felt more thoroughly satiated in her life. "I'm afraid I haven't been a very good hostess."

"Come again?"

She smiled. "I invited you up for coffee when I didn't have any, and I've neglected to offer you something to eat. Well," she amended naughtily, biting her lip, "other than me."

Victor laughed, a deep, husky rumble that made her insides clench. "Believe me, *cariño*," he murmured suggestively, "I can't think of anything I'd rather feast on than you."

She blushed deeply, burying her hot face against his chest. "I can't believe what we just did, Victor."

"Neither can I," he admitted, gently nuzzling her hair. "But I'm glad it happened. It was absolutely incredible."

"Out of this world." She sobered after a moment, lifting her head to meet his gaze. "But we didn't use protection."

Guilt flickered in his eyes. "I know," he said grimly, "and I'm really sorry. I never take risks like that. I got carried away, but that's no excuse for being irresponsible."

She smiled ruefully. "You weren't exactly alone. I was right there with you."

He cradled her cheek in his hand, searching her eyes. "Are you on the pill?"

She hesitated, then shook her head. "I'm not very... sexually active."

His expression gentled. "I know."

Heat stung her face. "What do you mean? Was it *that* obvious?"

He gave her a look. "That's not what I meant, and you know it."

She smiled shyly. "So what tipped you off to the fact that I, ah, don't get around much?"

"I have a sixth sense about these things."

"Of course," she muttered. "An experienced guy like you can probably spot a one-timer a mile away."

His brow lifted. "One-timer?"

She nodded slowly. "You're only the second man I've ever been with, Victor."

Tenderness softened his gaze. "Thank you," he said quietly.

"For what?"

"For entrusting me with your body. For giving me the incredible privilege of making love to you."

She swallowed hard, his heartfelt words touching a chord deep within her. Trying to play it off, she shrugged dismissively. "It was long overdue."

One corner of his mouth quirked. "I'm glad I was able to scratch your itch."

"Me, too." She grinned, sighing contentedly. "As for the other matter, I know my body like clockwork, and I'm not ovulating. So, um, we should be okay."

He nodded slowly. "Okay."

They gazed at each other for a prolonged moment before Victor gathered her close again. She snuggled against him, tucking her head beneath his chin as she ran her hand over the hard, muscled planes of his chest and abdomen. After reminding him what he'd told Bethany Dennison's little brother that day, she said teasingly, "Oh, yeah, Dr. Aguilar. You *definitely* need to hit the gym more often."

He chuckled softly.

Smiling whimsically, Tamara said, "Forgive my ignorance, but can you explain to me why you have two last names? Someone told me long ago, but I forgot how it works."

Victor sucked his teeth. "Typical gringa."

She retaliated with a sharp poke to his ribs that made him laugh. "Just kidding."

"Yeah, you'd better be." She grinned, watching as he captured her hand and gently nibbled on her fingertips, sending frissons of warmth down her spine.

"Okay, so here's how it works," he drawled. "In Colombia, as well as all Latin countries, most people have what we call two *apellidos,* which basically means a surname. Your first surname is your father's first surname. Your second is your mother's first surname—what Americans refer to as the maiden name. You follow?"

Tamara nodded. "I think so."

"So I'm Victor Aguilar García. Aguilar is my father's first surname, García is my mother's." He grinned lazily. "Many Latinos who immigrate to America drop the second name to make it less confusing for you gringos."

"Hey!" Tamara sputtered protestingly. "One more crack like that, and this *gringa* is tossing you out on your ass!"

Victor laughed, dragging her back into his arms and affectionately kissing the top of her head. "So feisty, woman."

"Whatever," she grumbled even as she nuzzled his throat, savoring the warm, musky scent of his skin. He stroked his fingers through her hair and gently massaged her scalp, drawing a contented purr out of her. She could have stayed in bed with him forever.

"So who was the lucky guy?" Victor murmured.

"Who?"

"Your first. Who was he?"

She sighed. "Someone I dated off and on during college and med school."

"That long?"

She nodded, wondering if she'd only imagined the jealous edge to his voice. "We were both consumed with becoming doctors, so we knew our relationship wasn't going anywhere. But whenever we, um, you know—"

"—had an itch that needed scratching?" Victor drawled wryly.

"Yes. Whenever we had needs, we knew we could count on each other to be there." She hesitated, then shrugged. "The arrangement worked for both of us."

"Hmm."

She angled her head back to look at Victor. "What does that mean?"

He met her gaze directly. "That may have worked for you back then, but it wouldn't now."

"You don't think so?"

"Nope. You want more out of a relationship, Tamara. And you deserve more."

She said nothing, neither confirming nor denying what he'd said.

"And if you think I'll settle for that kind of arrangement with you," he continued, his eyes boring into hers, "you'd better think again."

Tamara swallowed tightly. "Victor—"

He leaned down and kissed her, deeply and possessively.

After only a slight hesitation she melted, her arms curving around his neck as he rolled her gently onto her back. The scorching length of his erection pressed against her belly as he settled between her legs. She wrapped her thighs around his hips, shuddering as he rubbed the blunt head of his shaft up and down the tender folds of her sex.

Their eyes locked as he slowly slid into her, then pulled out halfway and thrust again.

As they began rocking together, she stared into his fiercely glittering eyes, and he stared back.

"Eres mía para siempre," he whispered.

You're mine forever.

Tamara shivered.

Because even if she hadn't understood his words, she still would have known that he'd just staked his claim to her.

Chapter 11

After a night of intensely passionate lovemaking, Tamara and Victor awoke early the next morning and took a long, steamy shower together.

Since Victor always kept a change of clothes and an extra set of scrubs in his duffel bag, he hadn't needed to return home to get dressed for work. So after Tamara whipped up some scrambled eggs and bacon, they sat down to eat at the breakfast table—the very same table they'd christened last night—and spent the entire meal exchanging heated looks and wicked grins.

On the way to the hospital, Tamara was surprised when Victor took a detour. Perched on the back of his Harley with her arms wrapped around his waist, she called out to him, "Where are we going?"

Glancing over his shoulder, he called back, "To look at something."

"What?"

"You'll see."

Ten minutes later, he steered into a gated community nestled along the banks of the Potomac River. Tamara watched, with mounting curiosity, as he used a key card to open the gate, then parked the Harley in an empty spot near the front of a luxury high-rise building.

"Whose key card was that?" Tamara asked as they climbed off the motorcycle.

Victor smiled enigmatically. "I'll tell you in a minute."

She eyed him suspiciously. "Why are you being so mysterious?"

His smile deepened. "Isn't that what women want? A man of mystery who holds your interest?"

Tamara grinned. As if *he'd* ever have to worry about any woman losing interest in him.

As they walked toward the building, she admired the lushly landscaped grounds and surrounding trees ablaze with fall color. "Gorgeous place," she remarked.

"Very."

"So again, I ask, what're we doing here? We have to be at work in half an hour."

"I know. This won't take long."

As they entered the elegant lobby, the front desk attendant glanced up. He took one look at their matching blue scrubs and smiled, either assuming that they could afford to live there, or had friends who did.

They rode the elevator to the top floor and got off, walking to a door at the end of the long, bright corridor. Once again, Tamara watched curiously as Victor punched numbers into the combination keypad, then met her gaze and grinned.

"*This* is what I wanted to show you," he said, and opened the door with a dramatic flourish.

Tamara stepped inside the empty condo, her eyes widening as she took inventory of a gleaming expanse of hardwood floors, a dramatic twelve-foot ceiling bordered by crown molding, and windows on a facing wall that commanded a breathtaking view of the Potomac River.

"Oh, my God," she breathed, turning slowly in a circle. "This place is amazing."

"Yeah," Victor agreed, sweeping an appreciative glance around. "It's even nicer than—"

"Oh, look at that!" Tamara squealed, racing across the room to admire a soaring limestone fireplace. She ran her hands over the mantel with a sigh of longing. "Man, I wish my apartment had a fireplace."

Victor snorted. "I wish this *was* my apartment."

"Whose is it?"

"You know Dr. Ambrose?"

Tamara ran through a mental Rolodex of doctors she'd encountered at the hospital, wrinkling her nose when the name registered. "Plastic surgeon? Drives the flashy red Ferrari? Walking poster child for narcissistic personality disorder?"

Victor laughed. "Damn, woman! You're brutal."

Tamara grinned impishly. "I call 'em like I see 'em. So this is Ambrose's crib?"

"Yeah. He just accepted a new position in Los Angeles—"

"Ah, yes. The Mecca for plastic surgeons."

"Right." Victor's mouth twitched at the not-so-subtle dig. "Anyway, as you can see, he's already vacated the premises. He wanted to sell his condo before he leaves, but he knows he won't get fair market value in this lousy economy. So he's decided to rent out the place instead. Yesterday he asked me if I was interested."

Tamara snorted, glancing around. "Who wouldn't be interested?"

Victor smiled. "I'm glad to hear you say that, because that's actually why I brought you here this morning."

Tamara eyed him warily as he sauntered toward her. "What are you talking about?"

"I want you to move in with me."

She gaped at him, convinced she'd heard wrong. "Excuse me?"

"Your ears aren't deceiving you. I want us to move in together."

"What? You can't be serious!"

He stopped in front of her, holding her stunned gaze. "I assure you that I'm very serious. Move in with me, Tamara."

She swallowed, her pulse thudding at the husky, intoxicating timbre of his voice. She took a step back, then another, needing as much distance between them as possible. "We can't move in together, Victor," she told him.

"Why not?"

"*Why not?* Because it's too soon! Yesterday we slept together, today we're moving in together. What's tomorrow? Getting engaged?"

A slow, lazy smile curved his mouth. "Are you proposing, *cariño?*"

Her heart lurched. "Of course not. Don't be ridiculous."

"Are you sure? Because I might be amenable to—"

She choked out a laugh. "I'm not proposing to you, Victor." But a strange wave of longing had swept through her at the thought of being his wife. Sharing a bed with him, sharing a home. Sharing his life.

Briskly she cleared her throat. "Look, the bottom line is, we can't move in together. Especially not here."

"Why not here?"

"Are you serious?" she demanded, gesturing expansively around the room. "Look at this place, Victor! It's a waterfront condo! Even splitting the rent, we couldn't possibly afford to live here. Ambrose must be paying at least three grand a month. So God only knows what he'd charge us."

"Fifteen."

Tamara's jaw dropped. "Did you say fifteen? As in *fifteen hundred?*"

"Yeah."

"Really? That's very generous of him." Her eyes narrowed suspiciously. "What's in it for him?"

Victor shrugged a broad shoulder. "He's looking out for a fellow Stanford alum, and he likes the peace of mind that comes with renting out his condo to someone he knows and trusts."

"Uh-huh." Tamara was skeptical. "What else?"

Victor grinned, playfully tweaking her nose. "Such a suspicious mind."

"Damn straight. So what's the story? Why's Ambrose giving you such a discount on the rent?"

"He sort of owes me a favor."

Tamara eyed him speculatively. "What kind of favor?"

"It's a long story."

"Oh, I see." She grinned knowingly. "You either covered for him with a patient—or a woman."

Victor rubbed his jaw, humor glinting in his eyes. "Let's just say he was very grateful for my, ah, assistance. The point is, the condo's mine if I want it. And I do. But only if you'll share it with me, Tamara. So what do you say?"

"I don't know, Victor." She was undeniably tempted to accept his offer. The condo was absolutely gorgeous, and the idea of living with him appealed to her more than she could have ever imagined. But she didn't know if she was ready to take that next step in their relationship. She hadn't even had time to adjust to them becoming lovers, although waking up in his arms that morning had felt as natural to her as breathing.

"If it's a roommate you want," she hedged, "I'm sure you'd have no problem finding—"

"I don't want a roommate." His voice deepened. "I want you."

Her belly quivered, and her pulse went haywire. "I—I don't know," she said again, scraping her hand through her hair as she began pacing the glossy floor. "I'd have to break my lease, and I wasn't planning to move anytime soon. My apartment suits my needs just fine—"

"You said you were overpaying for it," Victor reminded her. "If you moved in here with me, you'd probably end up saving money, because we would split the rent sixty-forty."

She shot him a surprised look. "You'd be willing to pay sixty percent?"

"Of course. And when we get our next salary increase, I'll pay even more."

Tamara stared at him, then shook her head quickly.

"I couldn't let you do that, Victor. You have more expenses than I do. You help support your family and—"

He held up his hand. "Let me worry about that. Just give me your answer."

She wavered, gnawing her lower lip. "How many bedrooms are there?"

"Two." His mouth quirked. "We could use the second for a study."

Tamara laughed. "Nice try, papi, but I'd want my own room."

He followed her into the gourmet kitchen, watching as she admired the custom cherry cabinets, granite countertops and stainless steel appliances.

"Do you like to cook?" he asked her.

"Not as much as I used to," she admitted. "Who has the time or energy to cook when you're working eighteen-hour days? That said, this kitchen would definitely inspire me."

Victor grinned. "Sounds good to me."

"Don't get any ideas about turning me into your domestic slave," she warned with a playful poke to his ribs, which made him laugh.

They explored the rest of the apartment, both impressed by the large bedrooms with great views, oversize closets, and the two bathrooms filled with travertine marble and quartz fixtures. Victor explained the amenities, which included a rooftop garden deck, fitness club and concierge service.

As they wandered back into the living room, Tamara sighed deeply. "I gotta hand it to Dr. Ambrose. He's got excellent taste."

"Of course," Victor drawled. "Would you expect anything less from a Ferrari-flaunting narcissist?"

They both laughed.

Walking over to the sun-drenched wall of windows, they gazed out at a sailboat drifting lazily across the Potomac River. Wrapping his arms around Tamara's waist, Victor leaned down and murmured into her ear, "Just imagine waking up to this view every day."

Tamara shivered, the hot silk of his voice caressing her skin and heating her blood. If they hadn't had to go to work, she would have gladly made love to him right then and there, on the floor of a virtual stranger's empty apartment.

"This is all very tempting," she admitted softly. "But I don't want to rush into anything."

"I know." Victor nuzzled her earlobe. "Just think about it. Okay?"

She nodded slowly. "Okay."

But she knew she'd already made up her mind.

Later that evening, Victor was resting in the on call room when he heard the door open and close quietly, followed by the soft click of the lock being turned.

Even before he opened his eyes and saw Tamara coming toward the bed, he knew it was her. His body had grown so attuned to her, he would have sensed her even if he were blindfolded and standing in the middle of a crowded arena.

He sat up halfway as she reached the bunk bed. "Hey," he whispered.

"Hey, yourself," she whispered back, climbing onto the bed and straddling his thighs. He grew instantly hard, his erection tenting the front of his scrubs.

Tamara laughed, a soft, naughty laugh that stole through the shadows like a fragrant curl of smoke. "I swore I'd never do this," she confessed, her breath fanning his face as her lips brushed his forehead.

Victor smiled dreamily. "Do what?"

"Hook up at work. It's so *Grey's Anatomy*-ish."

Victor chuckled as the tip of her tongue traced his lips before parting them. He shivered as she sensually licked the inside of his mouth while reaching down to cup the heavy ridge of his erection. He groaned thickly, closing his eyes.

She untied the drawstring of his scrub bottoms and reached inside his dark briefs. His breath hissed out as her fingers closed around his hard, throbbing shaft. She began caressing him slowly and provocatively, her hand sliding up and down his length until he thought he'd go insane. When she lowered her head and took him deep into her mouth, he snatched the pillow behind his head and pressed it over his face to muffle an agonized groan.

She licked over and around the sensitive head of his penis as her hand massaged his engorged sac. His heart pounded as his hips moved up and down, thrusting into the hot suction of her mouth. She knew just how to pleasure him using her lips, tongue and the inside of her cheeks to send jolts of ecstasy tearing through his body.

Knowing he was on the verge of exploding, he tossed aside the pillow and pulled out of her mouth. Her eyes danced with wicked laughter as he gripped her shoulders and flipped her onto her back. He made quick work of untying the drawstring of her scrubs and sliding them down her legs, followed quickly by her silk panties. The scent of her arousal went straight to his head, a powerful aphrodisiac. He pressed his palm against her hot mound and slid one finger inside her wetness. She arched upward on a low, sultry moan.

He removed his finger from her body and brushed her nectar over her lips, then leaned down and kissed her, unbearably aroused by the taste of her. Their tongues tangled and mated, an erotic glide of wet and heat.

Breaking the kiss, Victor reached down and scooped his wallet off the floor. After fumbling out a condom, he rolled the latex over his erection and settled between Tamara's warm thighs. When he stroked the head of his penis along her moist cleft, they both trembled with desire. She spread her legs wider, their gazes locking as he grabbed her hips and drove into her with one deep, powerful thrust. As she cried out softly, he shuddered at the feel of her hot, silky sheath enveloping him like a glove—one made just for him.

They quickly found their rhythm, the bed squeaking quietly beneath their thrusting bodies. They both knew the risk they were taking, knew there'd be hell to pay if they got caught. But Victor didn't care. He couldn't have stopped making love to Tamara if his life depended on it.

They kissed with their eyes open as they rocked together, driving each other closer and closer to the edge. When Victor reached between their joined bodies and fingered Tamara's swollen clit, she gasped into his mouth. He felt her body clench for a suspended moment. Seconds later, she began spasming and contracting around his shaft. As she climaxed, her head went back and her lips parted just as Victor reclaimed her mouth, swallowing her rapturous cry.

He sucked her tongue as he worked her quivering

insides, pumping harder and faster until his body exploded in an orgasm that had him shuddering and bucking violently against her.

For long moments afterward they clung to each other, her face pressed against his neck as their lungs heaved for air. Outside the room, they heard voices passing by the door.

"Do you think anyone heard us?" Tamara whispered breathlessly.

Victor grinned, kissing her damp nose. "Too late to do anything about it now."

Her eyes glittered with amused mischief. "Look what you've got me doing, sneaking off to have quickies when I'm supposed to be working."

His grin widened. "I always knew there was a bad girl hiding in there somewhere, just waiting to break loose."

Tamara chuckled. "Well, I'm locking her back up now, so say goodbye."

Victor kissed her softly, then winked. "*Adiós,* Naughty Tamara. Till we meet again."

As they sat up and began getting dressed, Victor said very casually, "I want you to meet my parents."

Tamara stared at him, her eyes widening with surprise. "Your…parents?"

"Yeah."

"Wow," she murmured, shaking her head at him. "First the apartment…now this. You don't waste any time, do you?"

"Not when I know what I want." Victor didn't care how he sounded. He was crazy about her and, premature or not, he was ready to take their relationship to the next level. Which was why he'd asked her to move in with him that morning. Seeing her every day at the hospital wasn't enough for him. He wanted more of her. He *had* to have more.

But Tamara was skittish, he reminded himself. So he had to tread with caution.

"Your mother's been to the hospital to visit you plenty of times, so I've met her before." He shrugged, feigning indifference. "Seems only right that you meet my parents."

Tamara was silent, her expression thoughtful as she redid her ponytail.

"There's a new French restaurant I've been hearing great things about," he continued in the same casual tone. "I can make reservations for Saturday since we're both off that evening. And I want you to bring your mother. My treat."

He found himself holding his breath, awaiting Tamara's response. She was no fool. She understood the magnitude of what he was asking of her, just as she'd understood that living under the same roof would make them more than roommates.

After what seemed an eternity, she whispered, "Okay."

Victor stared at her, heart thudding. "To which one?"

Looking him in the eye, she smiled. "Both."

Chapter 12

Tamara uncrossed and recrossed her legs, anxiously tapping her stiletto-clad foot in the air. Her stomach was a vicious tangle of nerves, leaving her slightly nauseous at the thought of consuming a meal. Which would be expected of her, considering that she was dining at a five-star restaurant.

Watching her daughter out of the corner of her eye, Vonda St. John murmured, "Lord have mercy. I haven't seen you this nervous and fidgety since the first day of kindergarten."

Tamara shot her mother a wry look. "I'm sure it's been more recent than that."

"I don't think so."

"No? I'm pretty sure I was a nervous wreck while I awaited my results from the MCAT, then waited to find out whether I'd gotten accepted into Dartmouth."

Her mother pursed her lips, striking a thoughtful pose. After another moment she shook her head. "Nope. Not even then." At Tamara's skeptical look, she elaborated, "You were nervous, sure, but you knew you'd aced the exam. And I never doubted that you'd get into Dartmouth, or any other medical school you applied to."

Tamara gave her a small, knowing smile. "You never doubt me."

"Which is why I know Mr. and Mrs. Aguilar are going to love you. How could they not?"

Tamara could think of one glaringly obvious reason, but she refrained from saying so. When she began gnawing her lower lip, Vonda clucked her tongue in exasperation.

"Stop doing that before you ruin your lipstick."

Tamara instantly released her lip, then covered her face with her hands and groaned softly. "What was I thinking, Ma? Why did I agree to meet Victor's parents?"

"You agreed because he asked you to," Vonda gently reminded her. "And the fact that he did tells me that he's very serious about you. Before tonight, I wasn't sure how serious *you* were about him. But now, seeing what a basket case you are over meeting his parents, I have my answer."

Tamara blushed, meeting her mother's quiet, discerning gaze. "It's only natural that I would want Mr. and Mrs. Aguilar to like me, Ma. We're about to spend an entire evening together. It's going to be pretty awkward if they decide right off the bat that they hate me."

"Of course." But the knowing gleam in Vonda's dark eyes let Tamara know that she saw right through her explanation.

Averting her gaze, Tamara glanced down anxiously at her wristwatch. "They're late. Maybe they decided not to come."

Vonda chuckled dryly. "Or maybe they're just operating on colored people's time."

For the first time that evening, Tamara laughed. "Then I guess we'll have something in common after all."

Vonda snorted. "Says who? *You've* never been late a day in your life. You arrived two weeks earlier than your due date, and every Sunday before church you were always dressed and ready to leave the house before *I'd* even gotten out of bed."

"Speaking of church," Tamara muttered darkly, eyeing the front entrance of the restaurant, "let Victor show up later than his parents, and he's gonna need some serious intercessory prayer after I get done with—" She broke off at the sight of him striding purposefully through the doors. She exhaled a sigh of relief. "There he is. Thank God."

Quickly she rose and hurried to meet him as he headed toward the plush waiting area. He looked devastatingly handsome in a charcoal dress shirt that was open to the strong column of his throat and accentuated his broad, muscular shoulders. Well-tailored black trousers hung low on his lean waist and rode his long legs to perfection. Though he'd gotten a fresh shave and a haircut, he still exuded an air of rakish dishabille that defied taming.

"Hey, baby." His warm lips claimed Tamara's in a brief but powerfully sensual kiss that promised more to come later. "Sorry I'm late," he murmured, smiling into her eyes. "I got held up."

"I figured as much," Tamara said, her anxiety momentarily forgotten in the face of his breathtaking virility. She stroked his smooth-shaven jaw, savoring the subtle, woodsy spice of cologne that wafted from his skin. "You clean up very nice, Dr. Aguilar."

"I was just thinking the same thing about you." His gaze ran the length of her, taking in her freshly relaxed hair, black sheath dress and strappy stiletto heels. His blue eyes glittered with unadulterated male appreciation. "You look absolutely stunning, *cariño*."

"Thank you," she said, her insides tingling with pleasure. "You know I had to represent."

"And you most certainly do." He smiled, affectionately touching her face before turning to greet her mother. "Hey, Ms. St. John," he said warmly, wrapping her in a bear hug. "How are you?"

"I'm doing just fine, Victor. It's wonderful to see you again."

"You, too." He drew back, giving her an admiring once-over before shaking his head. "I definitely see where your daughter gets her good looks from."

Tamara watched, with a mixture of incredulity and amusement, as her mother blushed and tittered like a schoolgirl. "Oh, hush. You're just being a charmer."

"Maybe," Victor drawled with a wink, "but it doesn't change the fact that you're a very beautiful woman, Ms. St. John."

Vonda laughed, her blush deepening as she shook her head sympathetically at Tamara. "No wonder he's got you wrapped around his finger."

"He does not," Tamara protested.

Victor and her mother traded conspiratorial grins.

The lighthearted moment was interrupted by the arrival of Victor's parents.

If Tamara thought she and *her* mother looked alike, they had nothing on Victor and his father, who were the spitting image of each other. Luis Aguilar was tall and broad-shouldered, with piercing blue eyes and thick, wavy hair that had turned mostly gray, giving him a sexy, distinguished appeal.

After Victor had exchanged affectionate greetings with his parents, he began the introductions. If Luis and Marcela were shocked to discover that their son's new girlfriend was African-American, they gave no indication as they smiled politely and shook Vonda's hand.

"And this is Tamara," Victor said, drawing her possessively to his side.

Tamara swallowed hard. "Hello, Mr. and Mrs. Aguilar," she said pleasantly, shaking their hands. "It's a pleasure to meet you."

"Hello, Tamara," they responded with smiles that seemed forced. And Tamara didn't miss the way Marcela's shrewd, assessing gaze raked over her before the edges of her mouth tightened with disapproval.

At that moment the maître d' materialized to escort them to a table tucked into a private corner of the elegant restaurant. After everyone had reviewed the leather-bound menus and ordered their entrées, Marcela's dark gaze settled on Tamara with an unerring directness that made her feel like prey caught in the crosshairs of a hunter's rifle scope. As if sensing her discomfiture, Victor reached under the table and gently took her hand, threading his strong fingers through hers.

"So, Tamara," his mother began conversationally,

"our Victor tells us that you are also an intern at the hospital."

"Yes, I am."

"Good for you." The woman paused. "We were surprised to learn that you have been there the whole time. Victor has never mentioned you before. He's talked about Ravi, the one whose parents are from India. And we've heard about Isabelle, the one who's going to be a pediatrician. But you, Tamara? Not a word about you."

"Oh, that's not surprising," Tamara drawled, exchanging wry glances with Victor.

"No?" Marcela looked askance at Vonda, who sat on the other side of her daughter. "Had you ever heard anything about Victor?"

"Yes." Vonda's mouth twitched. "But nothing that can be repeated in polite company."

Victor and Tamara laughed.

But Marcela was not amused. She frowned at Tamara. "Does that mean you and Victor didn't get along?"

"I'm afraid so," Tamara said with sham solemnity.

The woman's lips thinned with displeasure, as if she were offended by the notion of anyone having the audacity to differ with her son.

"So what changed?" Luis asked curiously, speaking for the first time since the waiter had taken their orders and departed. "How did the two of you go from being enemies to introducing each other to your families?"

Victor and Tamara gazed at each other. "Let's just say we came to our senses and realized that we have more in common than not," Victor murmured.

Tamara smiled, squeezing his hand beneath the table.

Vonda discreetly steered the conversation in a new

direction, asking Luis and Marcela about their respective jobs. Luis worked for Virginia's commuter rail system, while Marcela divided her time between answering phones in a county clerk's office and catering for parties and weddings on the weekends. The Aguilars were decent, hardworking people who'd scraped for every penny to provide for their children—just as Vonda had done for Tamara as a single mother.

As their parents talked, Tamara and Victor enjoyed their own private conversation—one that didn't necessarily require words. With her hand resting on Victor's hard thigh, Tamara could feel the flex and play of sinewy muscle every time he shifted in the chair. She found herself wishing that they were the only two at the table. If they'd been alone, she would have run her hand up his leg until she reached the thick bulge at his groin and stroked him until his erection strained against the zipper of his trousers.

As she unconsciously began kneading his thigh, the smoldering heat in Victor's eyes let her know that he, too, wished they could be alone.

They were so absorbed in each other that they didn't notice that the waiter had returned with their meals until Vonda pointedly cleared her throat and said humorously, "If the two of you want to eat at your own table—"

Grinning abashedly, Tamara and Victor pried their eyes away from each other to meet the waiter's amused gaze. He set their plates down with a flourish and topped off their wine, then asked whether they needed anything else before he glided away.

Draping a linen napkin across her lap, Tamara

glanced around the table at everyone's entrées. "Everything looks delicious," she enthused.

"Yes, indeed," Vonda agreed.

Luis and Marcela said nothing, dubiously eyeing their plates.

Tamara shot a nervous glance at Victor. Dining at the upscale French restaurant had been his idea, though he'd admitted that his parents rarely ventured beyond the spectrum of traditional Spanish cuisine they were accustomed to. *They need to start getting used to stepping out of their comfort zone,* he had insisted—a sentiment he'd also applied to his parents' need to accept his relationship with Tamara.

But judging by the way the couple was frowning at their food, Tamara wasn't very optimistic that *she* would fare much better in winning them over.

"Mmm," Victor murmured, sampling his *boeuf en croûte.* "That's good."

"It looks good," Tamara agreed.

"Here, try some."

He fed her a forkful of the succulent beef dish, staring at her mouth as she chewed. Out of the corner of her eye, she could see his mother watching them with unconcealed displeasure.

"Well?" Victor prompted softly.

"Delicious," Tamara murmured.

"Told you." Slowly he licked the fork and drew it into his mouth, as if he were savoring her taste. Heat pooled between Tamara's legs at the blatantly sensual gesture. When she glanced self-consciously at Marcela, the woman's eyes were narrowed to dangerous slits.

"How's yours?" Victor asked, drawing Tamara's gaze back to his face.

"My...?"

"Duck confit."

"Oh." She hadn't tasted it yet. Feeling discombobulated, she forked up a bite of the tender, flavorful meat. "Delicious."

"Are you going to offer me any?"

"I don't think that's a good idea," she muttered under her breath.

Victor chuckled quietly, seemingly unconcerned by his mother's death glare. Or so Tamara thought, until he met Marcela's eyes across the table and murmured something in Spanish. Though Tamara couldn't understand the words, she didn't need a translator to discern the understated menace in his deep voice.

Whatever he said brought an embarrassed flush to his mother's face. With obvious reluctance she lowered her gaze to her meal and began eating.

Tamara was grateful for the reprieve, though she suspected it wouldn't last very long.

She was right.

Ten minutes later, Marcela had her back in her crosshairs. "So tell me," she said, rudely interrupting Tamara's side conversation with her mother, "why do you want to be a surgeon?"

Before Tamara could respond, Victor drolly interjected, "For the same reason I do, Mama. She's a sadist who enjoys cutting people open and holding their hearts in the palm of her hand."

Vonda choked out a laugh. Even Luis ducked his head to hide a small smile.

But Marcela looked nauseated. She glanced down at her food with such distaste, Tamara would have sworn the plate was crawling with slimy worms and snails.

Thank God the woman hadn't ordered escargot from the menu.

"To answer your question, Mrs. Aguilar," Tamara said evenly, slapping Victor's thigh under the table, "I want to be a surgeon because I enjoy treating patients and making them well again."

"That's good." Marcela offered a thin smile. "I assume you don't want to get married or have any children, then."

Tamara gave her a startled look. "Why do you say that?"

The woman sighed. "Well, as you know, doctors have very demanding jobs. They work such long hours, and they're always on call—"

"Not always."

"Often enough." When Tamara didn't argue, Marcela continued smugly, "With such a busy schedule, when would you have time to tend to the needs of your husband and children?"

"I'll teach them to tend to their own needs," Tamara quipped lightly.

It was the wrong thing to say, she instantly realized, watching as Marcela traded an *I-told-you-so* glance with her husband, who'd remained conspicuously silent throughout the tense exchange.

"I was just joking, Mrs. Aguilar," Tamara hastened to explain. "What I meant to say is that I would find a way to balance the demands of my career with taking care of my family."

Marcela clucked her tongue. "You make that sound easy."

"Mama," Victor said, a low warning.

"No, let me respond." Tamara held his mother's

disapproving gaze. "I'm not trying to make anything sound easy, Mrs. Aguilar. Believe me, I *know* it won't be easy. But I certainly wouldn't be the first female doctor faced with the challenge of balancing work and family. Countless numbers of women face this reality every day, and somehow they manage to survive."

Marcela sniffed disdainfully. "*Surviving* isn't the same as *succeeding.*"

Tamara bristled, eyes narrowing. "I can't help but wonder, Mrs. Aguilar, whether you have the same concerns about your son becoming a doctor," she challenged. "Do you worry about him neglecting his wife and children?"

"Of course not."

"Really? And why not?"

Marcela frowned. "He's a man—"

"Didn't see *that* coming," Tamara muttered sarcastically.

Marcela ignored the barb. "Men are supposed to work hard to provide for their families. God made it that way."

"So what you're saying is that it's perfectly acceptable for men to be workaholics who neglect their families. But when women do the same thing, they're failures?"

Marcela smiled condescendingly. "I don't expect you to understand my viewpoint, Tamara. You come from a different generation, and your family background is not the same as mine."

"Meaning?"

"You were raised by a single mother—"

"—who worked damn hard to keep a roof over her head and food in her belly," Vonda interjected sharply.

"Of course you did." Marcela gave her a knowing look. "But you didn't have a choice, did you? There was no one else to do it."

Vonda's nostrils flared. After glancing at Tamara, she reached for her glass and took a long sip of wine, no doubt to calm her nerves.

"Mama," Victor challenged tersely, "how can you sit there and suggest that a woman's place is in the home when you've always worked at least two jobs to help support our family?"

"Not always, *mijo*," she countered. "Back in Colombia, my only job was to look after our home and take care of you and your brothers. It was only when we came to America that our circumstances changed, and I had no choice but to find outside work. But I don't expect you to remember that. You were too young." She gave him a gentle, maternal smile. "It's important for you to marry someone who will be around for you and your children. Someone who can manage the affairs of your household while you're at work."

"So that someone can't be a fellow doctor, right?" Tamara said sardonically.

"It would be a mistake." Marcela calmly met her gaze. "Unless you *want* your children to feel like orphans."

When Victor grimaced, Tamara thought he was reacting to his mother's statement—until she realized that her nails were digging into his thigh.

She sent him an apologetic glance as she relaxed her grip, appalled that she'd allowed his mother to get her so worked up. The woman was downright infuriating.

Marcela sighed, shaking her head at Tamara. "But we're getting ahead of ourselves, looking so far into the future when you haven't even gotten through your internship yet. I've seen firsthand how much hard work and sacrifice goes into completing the program. Victor tells us that some interns even end up quitting."

"Tamara won't be one of them," Vonda spoke up confidently. "She's always been at the top of her class, and she's never quit anything she started."

"That may be so," Marcela said casually, "but the program is very demanding. No one could blame Tamara for giving in to the pressure. Isn't that what happened to the other intern, the one who was caught stealing drugs from the hospital's pharmacy?"

"Mama," Victor growled warningly as Tamara's hackles went up.

She glared across the table at Marcela. "If you're referring to Terrence Matthews," she said tightly, "we're learning that he may have had a drug problem long before he arrived at Hopewell. If you're suggesting that *I* might be tempted to turn to drugs as a coping mechanism—and I won't speculate on your reasons for even making the comparison—you can just put your mind at ease. Because I have *every* intention of completing my residency and going on to become a successful cardiothoracic surgeon. But thanks for your concern."

Marcela frowned at her. "I wasn't trying to suggest that you would go down the same path as Terrence Matthews—"

"Of course you weren't," Tamara coolly interrupted. "After all, you have no way of knowing that Terrence just happens to be black. Oh, but wait. You *do* know, seeing as how his photo has been splashed all over the news for weeks."

Marcela sputtered with indignation. "How dare you

accuse me of such a thing? I never said a word about Terrence Matthews being black. *You* brought up his race, not me!"

"So I did," Tamara conceded, striving for patience. "Terrence and I are—were—among a handful of African-American interns at the hospital. So maybe I'm a little sensitive. But with all due respect, Mrs. Aguilar, I have a hard time believing you would have mentioned Terrence's drug problem in relation to me if I were Isabelle Morales."

Marcela's face reddened, and she pursed her lips so tightly they disappeared. She and Tamara glared at each other across the table, oblivious to everyone else.

"I see nothing wrong with pointing out how difficult the residency program can be—"

"I'm well aware of the challenges, thank you very much."

But Marcela wasn't finished. "If Terrence Matthews couldn't handle the pressure, and *he* came from a wealthy two-parent home—"

"Mama!" Victor barked.

But the damage had already been done.

Tamara looked at her mother, whose face was taut with suppressed anger. She'd been unjustly insulted, but she was holding her tongue for her daughter's sake.

With as much composure as she could manage, Tamara deliberately wiped her mouth with her napkin, dropped it onto the table and stood.

"I wish I could say it's been a pleasure to meet you, Mr. and Mrs. Aguilar," she said evenly, looking at each of them in turn, "but my mother always taught me not to lie. As a matter of fact, Mrs. Aguilar, my mother taught me a great deal about the importance of respect-

ing others and behaving with class—lessons *you* obviously would have benefited from. Enjoy the rest of your
evening."

"Carajo!" Victor swore viciously under his breath.
"Tamara, wait—"

But she and her mother were already striding away
from the table without a backward glance.

WHERE R U???

Tamara glanced at the latest text message from
Victor, scowled and tossed her cell phone down on her
mother's bed, where she'd been reclining for the past
hour.

Emerging from the master bathroom with a satin
scarf wrapped around her head and her face scrubbed
clean of makeup, Vonda asked wryly, "Another message from Victor?"

Tamara nodded shortly, still fuming over the way
the evening had ended. After she and her mother had
stormed off, Victor had caught up to them, apologizing
profusely for his mother's behavior and imploring them
to return to the table. Tamara had adamantly refused,
and when the valet brought her mother's car around,
she'd climbed behind the wheel and sped off before
Victor could stop her. She'd ranted and raved all the
way to her mother's single-story rambler in Fort Washington, flying across the Woodrow Wilson Bridge and
racing down the beltway until Vonda—gripping the
door handle for dear life—begged her to slow down.

Now, two glasses of Merlot later, Tamara's temper
had abated only slightly.

Lowering herself onto the queen-size bed, Vonda
picked up her daughter's cell phone and checked the

recent call history. "Four missed calls. Six text messages. All from Victor." She frowned and set down the phone, watching Tamara channel-surf with the same angry intensity she'd unleashed upon the road. "He's been camped outside your apartment, waiting for you to come home. You should at least let him know where you are."

"He knows where I am," Tamara grumbled darkly. "He just doesn't know how to get here."

Vonda sighed. "Maybe it wasn't such a good idea for me to be unlisted."

"It was an excellent idea," Tamara countered crisply. "How else could you have gotten all those rabid bill collectors to stop harassing you while you worked toward paying off your debt?"

Vonda grimaced at the memory. "Thank God those days are over."

"Amen. Now you've got perfect credit, you make good money *and* you love your job at the Pentagon. If you'd just accept a date from that tall, dark and handsome commander who's been asking you out for months, all would be right with the world."

Vonda scowled. "I have no interest in going out with that arrogant man. And don't try to change the subject. We were talking about you and Victor." She paused. "Maybe I should just call him and give him my address."

"You'll do no such thing, Ma," Tamara warned, grabbing her cell phone off the bed before her mother could reach for it. "Victor doesn't need to come over here. I have nothing to say to him."

"Don't you think it's a little unfair to punish him for the way his mother behaved?"

Tamara didn't answer, her angry gaze focused on the images flashing across the plasma television screen.

"Give me that," Vonda muttered, snatching the remote control out of Tamara's hand. "You're making me dizzy with all that channel changing."

Tamara heaved a frustrated breath, flopped back against the headboard and grabbed the pint of Häagen Dazs ice cream melting on the nightstand. The chocolate chip cookie dough, while her favorite flavor, was a sorry substitute for the crème brûlée she'd intended to order for dessert.

Shoving a creamy spoonful into her mouth, she mumbled disconsolately, "This isn't the way this evening was supposed to turn out."

"I know," Vonda murmured sympathetically.

"Victor's mother wasn't supposed to be such a barracuda. And a racist, on top of that."

Vonda frowned. "I *was* pretty shocked and disappointed by some of the things she said."

"And what about Victor's father?" Tamara burst out with renewed indignation. "I still can't believe he just sat there and let her run her mouth like that! But I guess he must have agreed with everything she said."

"Not necessarily." Vonda paused, lips pursed in thought for a moment. "I could be wrong, but I got the impression that he's not as opposed to your relationship with Victor as his wife is."

Tamara scowled. "Then why didn't he say anything?"

Vonda shrugged. "Maybe he doesn't want to argue with her. Maybe the man just wants some peace and quiet in his home."

Tamara snorted derisively. "Peace and quiet with *that* woman? I don't think so."

Her mother chuckled, turning off the television and setting down the remote control on her side of the bed—away from Tamara. "To be honest with you, there's a part of me that wants to give Marcela the benefit of the doubt, because I truly believe she just wants what's best for her son."

Tamara held up a hand. "Please don't defend that woman, Ma. Not after the way she insulted you tonight."

"I'm not defending her," Vonda said grimly. "Believe me, I wanted nothing more than to go off on her tonight, and the next time something like this happens, the gloves are coming off."

"Oh, there won't be a next time," Tamara said unequivocally. "If I never see Mrs. Aguilar again, it'll be too soon."

"Really?" Vonda slanted her a vaguely amused look. "And how do you intend to pull that off, considering that the woman will probably end up being your mother-in-law?"

Tamara froze, a spoonful of ice cream halfway to her mouth. She stared at her mother. "Wh-what do you mean?"

Vonda gave her an indulgent smile. "Isn't that what tonight was about? The introduction to the parents? Getting us accustomed to the idea of you two as a couple? Why else would you and Victor go to all the trouble if you weren't already planning to take the next big step in your relationship?"

"We're not planning anything," Tamara said hastily, setting aside the ice cream. "We just thought…well, since we're both so close to our parents, we just thought it would be nice for everyone to be on friendly terms with one another."

"Um-hmm." Vonda wasn't buying the explanation for a second. "I think you and Victor knew what you were doing when you arranged this special dinner. And that's perfectly fine with me, considering what I saw tonight when I looked at the two of you."

Tamara was almost afraid to ask. "What did you see?"

Vonda smiled. "For starters, I saw two young, brilliant doctors who have realized that there's even more to life than pursuing and achieving their career goals. I saw two people who share so much chemistry, I kept waiting for the restaurant to catch on fire. *Whew!*"

Tamara blushed deeply, making her mother laugh.

"You don't have to be embarrassed, baby. You were always so focused on your academics that boys were reduced to an afterthought. But I knew that would change when the right one came along." Vonda's eyes twinkled. "I'm glad you've met someone who rocks your world, which Victor clearly does."

Tamara laughingly groaned, covering her hot face with her hands. "If Mrs. Aguilar could have banished me to the other side of the restaurant—hell, to the other side of the world—I know she would have."

"Of course. She's not blind. She saw exactly what I saw tonight, and I suspect that's why she came out swinging like an animal backed into a corner." Vonda's voice softened. "But try as she might, she can't fight the inevitable."

Slowly Tamara removed her hands from her face

and met her mother's quiet, knowing gaze. "The inevitable?"

Vonda nodded. "You and Victor love each other. If you're willing to risk the scrutiny of your colleagues and incur the wrath of his mother, then you're serious about being together. So that means—"

"No," Tamara interrupted glumly, shaking her head. "I know what you're going to say, Ma, and you're usually right about things. But not this time."

Vonda frowned. "Are you saying that you and Victor *don't* love each other?"

"No. I mean, I—" Tamara heaved a shaky breath, shoving her hand through her hair. "I *do* love him," she admitted.

"And he loves you. Surely you must know that."

"I don't. Not really. I mean, he hasn't actually come out and said it."

"Have *you?*" Vonda countered pointedly.

Tamara hesitated, then shook her head. "But it doesn't really matter anymore. Victor and I won't work. I mean, I thought the biggest challenge we would face was getting in trouble at work for violating the hospital's nonfraternization policy. But after what happened tonight, I realize that we have even bigger obstacles to overcome, and I'm not so sure we can."

"If you love each other," Vonda said sagely, "you can overcome anything."

Tamara's heart constricted painfully. "I wish I believed that, Ma. But Victor is very close to his family. He sets aside money every month to help take care of his brothers, and his parents really depend on him. If Mrs. Aguilar refuses to accept our relationship, Victor will be devastated. I can't ask him to choose me over his family."

"You won't have to ask him," Vonda said with quiet certainty. "If that man loves you as much as I think he does, nothing will keep him from being with you. Nothing. And no one."

Chapter 13

Victor was still seething with fury when he arrived at his parents' house that evening, making it there in record time. Roaring into the driveway, he killed the engine and knocked the kickstand down with his foot, then lunged from the Harley and stalked to the front door.

Using his spare key, he let himself into the house and marched through the foyer to reach the living room. His brothers were all there. Alejandro was stretched out across the loveseat, long legs dangling over the arm as he laughed and talked softly on his cell phone. Christian and Fernando were sprawled on the sofa watching television, while Roberto lay on his stomach on the floor playing games on Alejandro's laptop.

They glanced up in surprise at Victor's appearance, their features so similar that for a moment Victor felt as if he were seeing a slideshow of himself at his brothers' ages—fourteen, sixteen, seventeen and nineteen.

"Hermanote," Christian greeted him with the familiar Spanish nickname for a big brother—a word he'd picked up from some Mexican friends. "What're you doing home?"

"Came to see our parents."

"Didn't you just have dinner with them?"

Ignoring the question, Victor walked over to Alejandro, removed a crisp fifty from his wallet and held it out to him.

Alejandro eyed the money quizzically. "What's this for?"

"Take your brothers out for some pizza or something."

"We already ate."

"Eat again. I need to talk to Mama and Papa in private."

Comprehension filled Alejandro's eyes. "Let me call you back, Amani," he murmured into the phone before snapping it shut and sitting up. He gave Victor a long, knowing look. "You're here about Tamara, aren't you?"

Victor nodded tightly.

"Yeah. I could tell by the way Mama and Papa looked that things didn't go too well over dinner. They've been holed up in their bedroom ever since they got home." Alejandro grimaced, then took the money from Victor. "I don't know if this will be enough. Have you seen the way these pigs eat?"

"Look who's talking!" Fernando protested.

Victor impatiently peeled off another twenty.

"Muchas gracias." Alejandro gleefully pocketed the

money, then paused. "I can't remember if I have any gas in my—"

Victor growled something obscene that made Alejandro laugh, holding up his hands in mock surrender. "Can't blame a guy for trying."

"Even if he gets his ass kicked in the process."

Alejandro grinned, rising from the loveseat to corral his younger brothers. "Come on, *hermanitos.* Victor needs to have a powwow with the old folks."

"About what?" Christian and Fernando asked curiously.

"Don't worry about it," Victor retorted.

"When we get back," Roberto asked him, "wanna play MLB 2K11 with me?"

Victor ruffled his baby brother's hair. "Maybe next time."

As the four siblings headed out the front door, laughing and talking boisterously among themselves, Luis and Marcela emerged from their upstairs bedroom, alerted by the commotion.

"Where's everyone going?" Marcela wondered aloud, tugging the lapels of her robe together as she descended the stairs. "Jandro didn't say he was taking his—" She broke off, her eyes widening in surprise when she saw her eldest standing at the bottom of the staircase. "Victor?"

"We need to talk," he said curtly.

His parents followed him into the living room and sat on the checkered sofa, watching as he began pacing the floor.

"Let me start off by saying that you owe Tamara and her mother an apology. Especially you, Mama."

Luis and Marcela exchanged indignant glances. "An

apology?" Marcela sputtered. "*They're* the ones who walked out on dinner with us. That was very rude—"

"Rude?" Victor echoed in disbelief, glaring at her. "After the way you insulted and demeaned them, you have the audacity to call *them* rude? I wouldn't have blamed either of them for walking out on you sooner!"

Marcela gasped, recoiling as if she'd been struck. "How can you say such a thing to me? I was only trying to get to know Tamara!"

"Get to know her?" Victor thundered furiously. "Are you serious, Mama? You weren't trying to get to know her. You were trying to humiliate her and provoke her into an argument so that you'd feel justified in saying that she's not good enough for me!"

"She's *not* good enough for you!"

"Why?" Victor challenged, anger and frustration driving twin fists into his stomach. "Because she's black?"

Marcela's face reddened. "I didn't say that!"

"You didn't have to! Everyone at that table knew exactly why you had such a problem with Tamara. *¡Ay Dios Mio!* The waiter probably even knew!"

"*Me importa un carajo!*" Marcela fired back. "I don't give a damn what anyone else thought!"

"Obviously not, or you wouldn't have behaved so deplorably!"

With tempers and emotions running high, they lapsed into rapid-fire Spanish, neither having the patience to accommodate the slower pace of English.

"I don't understand where your father and I went wrong," Marcela ranted, wringing her hands in consternation. "Even after we left Bogotá, we made sure you and your brothers would never forget where you came from. We moved into a community filled with other Colombians. We made you speak only Spanish at home. You attend the *quinceañeras* and parties and weddings of Colombians all the time! So is it asking too much for you to fall in love with a nice Colombian girl like Natalia?"

"Natalia?" Victor jeered.

"Yes, Natalia!"

"Let me tell you something about that 'nice Colombian girl' you're so enamored of, Mama. Barely an hour after I first met her, she put her hand down my pants and offered to give me a blowjob. Three hours later she was doing that, and then some."

"Victor!" Marcela gasped, clapping a hand to her mouth.

"Mijo," his father said warningly.

But Victor wasn't finished. "Do you know how many lovers Tamara had before me?" He held up a finger. "One, Mama. *One.* Now ask Natalia how many different men come and go from her apartment on a weekly basis."

His mother looked so shocked and scandalized that Victor felt a stab of guilt. He knew he'd probably burn in hell for talking to her in such a crass, disrespectful manner. But after the way she'd conducted herself tonight, he didn't give a damn. He was fed up with her putting Natalia on a pedestal. Enough was enough.

"I've known Tamara for more than a year," he continued relentlessly. "We recently got stranded overnight at the hospital. We spent an entire night alone in the same room, and not once did Tamara try to seduce me, even though we're very attracted to each other. You want to talk about *nice* girls, the kind you can bring home to your parents? Tamara is a nice girl, Mama. Not Natalia. *Tamara.* So let's set the record straight right now!"

Marcela sank back against the sofa cushion, her hand trembling as she sketched a sign of the cross over her chest. "Why are you doing this to me, Victor?" she complained bitterly.

"What am I doing to you, Mama? Aren't you the one who recently told me that my happiness is important? Didn't you encourage me to bring home someone I found special?" His lips twisted mockingly. "Or did that only apply to Colombian women?"

His mother gave him a beseeching look. *"¡Ay mijo!* Don't be that way, Victor. I saw the way you and Tamara were looking at each other tonight. No one is saying you can't take her to bed. You're a healthy young man with needs, and she is a beautiful girl. I know every man likes to try something different and exotic—"

Victor eyed her incredulously. "You think I'm just *experimenting,* Mama? You think Tamara's just a novelty to me?"

"Of course!"

"Well, you're wrong!"

Marcela stared up at him, her eyes wide with dread. *"Mijo—"*

"I love her, Mama. Do you understand? I *love* her. Even though we've only just started dating, I've asked her to move in with me. I want to marry her and come home to her every day. I want to have beautiful brown babies with her, and I hope to God we have a daughter who looks just like her." He paused meaningfully. "Does any of that sound like I'm just experimenting?"

His parents exchanged stunned glances.

"I'm going to be with Tamara," Victor told them, his voice etched in steel. "With or without your approval."

Marcela bowed her head and closed her eyes, as if she were praying for strength—or divine intervention. Luis rubbed her back consolingly, looking at Victor.

"You have to understand where we're coming from, *mijo*," he said with quiet gravity. "We didn't see this coming. All along you've been saying that you want to concentrate on finishing your residency before you think about marriage. And then, just a few days ago, you tell us about a woman you want us to meet. A woman we've never even heard of before. This is a lot for us to digest at once."

"I understand that, Papa," Victor said in a more conciliatory tone. "Believe me, I didn't see any of this coming, either. Honestly, even with having such positive role models as you and Mama, I didn't think it was possible for me to love any woman as much as I love Tamara."

His father searched his eyes for several moments, then gave an imperceptible nod of understanding.

His wife, in contrast, crossed her arms mutinously over her chest and glared at Victor. "Don't expect me to accept Tamara into this family. Because I won't, Victor. Do you hear me? *I won't!*"

Victor regarded his mother for a long, tense moment, then shook his head in disappointment. "I'm really sorry you feel that way, Mama. I was hoping to get through to you—"

"Get through to me? You're the one who's making a terrible mistake, *mijo!*"

Victor clenched his jaw, his expression hardening. "I

love you, Mama," he said, low and controlled, "but remember that I can be just as stubborn as you are. Don't force me to choose between you and Tamara, because I promise you won't like my decision."

With a brusque nod at his father, he turned and stalked out of the house.

Chapter 14

Two days later, Victor was standing at the empty nurses' station reviewing patient charts when a newcomer's voice drawled, "You know, I hate clichés."

Victor glanced around to find Dr. Balmer standing beside him at the counter. "Sorry. What did you say?"

"I said I hate clichés."

"What do you mean?"

"I mean just what I said. I hate clichés, Dr. Aguilar, and that's exactly what you and Dr. St. John have become."

Victor frowned at her. "I don't understand."

"Two wannabe heart surgeons who can't even diagnose the needs of your own heart." She snorted, shaking her head. "Makes no damn sense."

"It's complicated," Victor mumbled.

"So is cardiothoracic surgery," Balmer pointed out,

"but that didn't stop you from choosing it as your specialty."

Victor said nothing, returning to his paperwork.

"Everyone has noticed the way you and Dr. St. John have been avoiding each other—"

"Actually," Victor said darkly, "*she's* been avoiding me."

"Which is downright ludicrous, considering the way she went to bat for you last week."

Victor stopped writing. Lifting his head, he stared at his supervisor. "What do you mean she went to bat for me?"

Balmer arched a brow. "You didn't know? Last week when she found out that Dr. Dudley was considering whether to take disciplinary action against you, she marched right up to his office to talk him out of it."

Heart thudding, Victor eyed Dr. Balmer skeptically. "She did that?"

"Yup. Shocked the hell out of Dudley, too. She told him that you were the best intern out of your group—"

"What?"

"—and informed him in no uncertain terms that he'd be making a terrible mistake if he kicked you out of the program."

Victor was floored. He'd had no idea that Tamara had gone to the chief of staff to plead his case. He'd accused her of being a conformist and having no backbone, yet there she was, putting her neck on the line for him. It was one of the most unselfish things anyone had ever done for him. He was incredibly touched, and humbled beyond words.

Watching his stunned reaction, Balmer smiled softly.

"Do you know what else she told Dr. Dudley? She told him that you make her a better doctor."

"She said that?" Victor murmured, husky with emotion.

"She did. And I'm inclined to agree with her. I think you both bring out the best in each other."

Victor swallowed tightly.

"Now, I don't know whether or not she changed Dr. Dudley's mind," Balmer continued. "Truth be told, I don't think he was ever serious about kicking you out of the program anyway. Not when we're already under so much scrutiny, and not when he knows you're one of our most promising interns. But I can definitely tell you that Dr. St. John's visit had an impact on him. He told me that in all the years he's worked at this hospital, he's never seen an intern go to bat for a rival intern the way Dr. St. John did for you." She chuckled wryly. "Of course, now you've got him speculating about the nature of your relationship—"

At that moment, Tamara emerged from a patient's room down the hallway. When she glanced up from the chart she'd been reviewing and saw Victor standing at the nurses' station, she slowed her steps, then abruptly reversed course and headed in the opposite direction.

"We've got a runner," Balmer intoned humorously.

Victor swore under his breath. "Would you excuse me for a moment?" Without awaiting his supervisor's assent, he left his paperwork on the counter and strode purposefully after Tamara.

"Make it quick," Balmer called after him. "We're trying to run a hospital here, not a relationship counseling service!"

Victor's determined, ground-eating strides enabled him to catch up easily to Tamara. "We need to talk."

She shook her head, her charts clutched to her chest. "I have patients to see, and so do y—"

Spying the door to another supply closet—*perfect timing!*—Victor grabbed Tamara's arm and dragged her inside, kicking the door shut behind them.

She heaved an exasperated breath. "Really, Victor, this is becoming a rather bad habit—"

He didn't let her finish. Cupping her face between his hands, he crushed his lips to hers, swallowing her startled gasp. When she dropped her charts on the floor, he pushed her back against the door, pinning her with his body. She made a helpless little sound in her throat, a sound of surrender that ignited his blood. As her arms went around his neck, he devoured her mouth, pouring all of the love, passion and gratitude he felt into a hot, searing kiss that left them trembling and clutching each other.

"I know what you did for me," Victor whispered, running his lips along the satin arch of her throat. "I know you talked to Dr. Dudley to keep me in the program."

"I don't know what you're—" Tamara broke off with a soft moan as he nipped the pulse beating frantically at the base of her throat.

"You can't lie to me, *cariño.* I know your secret. You stood up to Dudley. You risked getting on his bad side just to protect me."

"Don't make such a big deal over it. This place would be dull without you."

"Liar," he murmured, sucking gently at the pulsing nerve in her throat. "You talked to him because you care what happens to me. Why? Because you care about me more than you're willing to admit, even to yourself."

"I do care about you," she whispered, her fingers tangling in his hair as she brushed tender kisses across his temple. "But it doesn't matter, Victor. We can't be together."

"The hell we can't," he growled, rolling his hips against her, making her body arch. "We're already together, and I intend to keep it that way."

"But your parents—"

He lifted his head, pinning her with a fiercely intent gaze. "Maybe you didn't hear me the first time. We're together, Tamara, and I intend to keep it that way."

She tenderly framed his face between her hands. "I want to be with you, Victor. God knows I do. But I don't think I can handle all the drama with your parents. And I don't want to come between you and them."

"You're not coming between anyone. I've already told my parents what I want, and now the ball's in their court. But I'm not waiting around for them to come to their senses. I'm moving on, Tamara, and if you think I'm letting you go without a fight, you'd better think again."

She gazed at him. "Victor—"

"I put down the security deposit for the condo, so we can move in whenever we're ready. The sooner, the better."

She hesitated, her dark eyes probing his. "Are you sure about this?"

"I've never been more sure of anything in my life."

"You don't think we're moving too fast?"

"Right now, sweetheart, I don't think we're moving fast enough."

She grinned, shaking her head in exasperation.

"So what do you say?" he prompted.

She bit her lip, still wavering. "I don't know...."

"Say yes."

"Victor—"

"Say yes," he warned, a wicked grin curving his mouth, "or I'm getting down on my knees, pulling down your pants, and burying my mouth between your legs. And when I make you scream—"

"Okay! Okay!" she relented hoarsely. When she shuddered against him and closed her eyes for a moment, Victor was sorely tempted to make good on his threat anyway.

He leaned down, nibbling her lush bottom lip as he smiled into her eyes. "Okay what?"

"Okay, I'll move in with you. *Sheesh.*"

"Good." He stroked his tongue over her lip, felt her shiver with arousal as his own body hardened. He toyed with the drawstring of her scrub bottoms. "Maybe we could just hang out here a lit—"

"Oh, no, you don't," she warned, shoving him back before dropping quickly to the floor and scooping up her fallen charts. She stood and opened the door, checked the empty hallway, then darted out of the closet before Victor could stop her.

He chuckled softly as he watched her go, consoling himself with the reminder that once they were living under the same roof, he'd have her whenever he wanted her.

Which would be pretty much all the time.

Chapter 15

Tamara removed a carton of milk from Victor's refrigerator and sniffed at the opening, her nose wrinkling in disgust.

"Does this man ever throw *anything* away?" she muttered, pouring the spoiled milk down the drain and chucking the empty carton into a large trash bag teeming with other junk she'd already discarded.

Over the past few days, she and Victor had been helping each other pack their belongings in preparation for Saturday's move. Since Tamara had gotten off from work earlier than him that evening, she'd driven over to his apartment to get a head start on cleaning out his refrigerator, which he'd sheepishly warned her was a mess.

He hadn't exaggerated. Though the rest of his sparsely furnished apartment was surprisingly neat, the refrigerator was crammed with old take-out containers, moldy vegetables and other items that had long since passed their expiration date.

As Tamara reached for a cloudy jar of pickles, the doorbell rang.

Shaking her head in amused exasperation, she closed the refrigerator and left the small kitchen to answer the front door.

"Don't tell me you lost your key before we've even—" She broke off, the teasing admonition dying on her lips when she found herself staring at an attractive young blonde leaning seductively on the doorjamb, her silk blouse unbuttoned to reveal her ample cleavage.

"May I help you?" Tamara asked coolly.

"Um." Straightening from the doorjamb, the woman checked the number on the door as if to confirm she had the right apartment. "I'm looking for Victor."

"He's not here."

"Ohhhkay. Do you know when he'll be back?"

"I'm sorry, what was your name again?"

"Natalia. I'm his neighbor."

Judging by the way she'd been posing in the doorway, Tamara thought darkly, she was—or had been—a hell of a lot more than Victor's neighbor.

Glancing down at the rubber gloves Tamara wore, Natalia chuckled softly. "I see he finally decided to hire a maid service. Good for him."

Tamara bristled. "I'm not his maid."

Natalia frowned. "You're not his—"

"No."

Coolly appraising green eyes looked Tamara up and down, taking in her fitted pink tee, denim skirt and bare feet. "Oh, I see," Natalia said with an understanding nod. "You must be Victor's new roommate, then. Something else he once talked about get—"

"I'm not his roommate." Tamara paused. "Not yet, anyway."

Natalia's eyes narrowed on hers. "I'm sorry," she said tightly, "I didn't catch your name."

"Tamara."

"And you are...?"

None of your damn business. "Look, I was in the middle of something, so I'll let Victor know you stopped by."

As Tamara moved to close the door, Natalia blurted out, "Would you mind if I wait for him?"

Tamara frowned. "Actually, I—"

"Here's the thing," Natalia interrupted, looking sheepish. "There's a maintenance man inside my apartment doing some work. I'm always uncomfortable with having strangers in my home while I'm there. You know, being a single woman living alone." She eyed Tamara imploringly. "Can I just hang out here until he's finished? I'll stay out of your way, I promise."

Tamara hesitated for several moments, then opened the door wider and stepped aside.

"Thanks." Natalia sashayed into the apartment and stopped short, her eyes widening with shock as she glanced around at all the cardboard boxes. "Wait a minute. Is Victor moving?"

"Yes."

Natalia gaped at her. "When?"

Ignoring the question, Tamara gestured vaguely to the sofa. "Make yourself comfortable. Like I said, I was in the middle of doing something."

Natalia followed her into the kitchen. "Are you and Victor moving in together?"

"We are, as a matter of fact."

"I didn't even know he was dating anyone!"

The woman's possessive tone set Tamara's back teeth on edge. Her task forgotten, she leaned against the counter and folded her arms across her chest. "Is there something I should know about you and Victor?"

Natalia smirked. "Other than the fact that we used to sleep together?"

"Yes." Tamara kept her expression neutral. "Other than that."

Natalia shrugged, flashing more cleavage with the gesture. "What did he tell you about me?"

"Nothing," Tamara said blandly. "He's never mentioned you at all."

Hurt flickered in the other woman's eyes, but she recovered quickly enough to retort, "Then I guess he's been keeping us a secret from each other, because I've never heard of you, either."

Tamara just looked at her.

A malicious gleam lit Natalia's eyes. "So I guess that means he didn't tell you that I met his parents?"

Tamara congratulated herself for not flinching, though she was stung to hear that she wasn't the only woman Victor had introduced to his parents. He'd led her to believe that she was special, and she'd foolishly fallen for it.

Natalia sighed contentedly. "Mr. and Mrs. Aguilar are such sweet, wonderful people. They were so excited when they found out that my family's also from Bogotá. Can you believe that Victor and I were born in the same town? What are the odds?"

"Indeed," Tamara murmured.

"They positively *adored* me," Natalia continued, twisting the knife deeper. "And, of course, the feeling was definitely mutual. Have you met Victor's parents, Tamara?"

She forced a smile. "Oh, yes, I've had the pleasure."

Natalia gave her a deliberate once-over, her eyes glimmering with laughter. "I bet *that* was an interesting meeting."

Before Tamara could respond—not that she even knew how to—they heard the jangle of keys outside the front door. They looked through the open entryway to watch as Victor stepped into the apartment, channeling Ricky Ricardo as he called out in a thickly accented voice, "Lucy, I'm home!"

He turned from closing the door, then froze at the sight of Tamara and Natalia emerging from the kitchen. He divided a wary glance between them. "What's up?"

Folding her arms across her chest, Tamara said with exaggerated sweetness, "Hey, honey. Look who dropped by."

His gaze shifted reluctantly to Natalia. "Hey."

"Hey, yourself," she said, her voice laced with petulant accusation. "You didn't tell me you were moving."

He cocked an amused brow. "Should I have?"

"It would have been nice. I go away for five days on a business trip, and I come back to learn that you're moving *and* you have a girlfriend."

Slowly, deliberately, Victor set his helmet down on the stack of cardboard boxes pushed against the wall near the door. Tamara didn't miss the way Natalia's predatory gaze devoured him, nor could she really blame her. She'd worked with Victor for more than a year, and her hormones still reacted to the sight of him in scrubs with those big black boots.

As she and Natalia watched, he sauntered across the room toward them. Stopping in front of Tamara, he leaned down and brushed his mouth over hers. Her pulse quickened, and heat pumped through her veins.

Bringing his warm lips to her ear, he murmured, "I could get very used to this."

She shivered. "What?"

"Coming home to you every day."

She couldn't suppress a pleased smile. Out of the corner of her eye, she could see Natalia glaring at them.

Holding Tamara's gaze, Victor drawled lazily, "Was there anything else you wanted, Natalia?"

"I guess not," she retorted sulkily.

"Well, then…thanks for stopping by."

She hesitated, then huffed out a breath and stomped out of the apartment, slamming the door behind her.

In the ensuing silence, Tamara and Victor stared at each other.

"Sorry about that," he murmured.

"Don't be. Natalia and I had a very enlightening conversation before you got home."

His eyes narrowed. "Enlightening?"

"Yup." Tamara turned away, walking back into the kitchen.

Victor followed her. "What did she tell you?"

"What do you think she told me?"

"I'm sure she told you that we slept together."

"Of course."

He sighed. "I've never claimed to be a monk—"

"I know." Tamara's tone was mild. "I'm not mad

because you slept with Natalia. She's a sexy woman. You'd have to be a monk *not* to have slept with her."

"So what are you mad about?"

"Who says I am?" she countered, opening the refrigerator and removing the cloudy jar of pickles.

"Come on, Tamara. I can tell you're upset about something. What else did she say to you?"

"I'd rather not—"

Victor took the jar from her hand and set it down on the counter, then took her chin between his thumb and forefinger and tipped her face up, forcing her to meet his probing gaze. "Tell me what's wrong."

"She said she met your parents, and they adored her." Tamara searched his eyes. "Is that true?"

Victor hesitated, then nodded reluctantly. "They were happy because Natalia's from Colombia. But that was last year, and I only slept with her a few times. She didn't mean anything to me."

Tamara frowned. "She must have meant *something* if you took her home to meet your parents."

"That's not how it happened. I didn't take her home. She was over here one day when they dropped by for a surprise visit."

"Oh." A wave of relief swept through Tamara. "I thought—"

"No," Victor said softly, holding her gaze. "You're the first woman I've ever wanted to introduce to my parents."

She smiled ruefully. "And look how well *that* turned out."

His expression clouded.

Although he'd told her that he was moving on, she knew his mother's rejection hurt him just as much as it hurt Tamara. It had been nearly a week since the disastrous dinner with his parents, and Marcela was still giving them the silent treatment. If she was even half as stubborn as her son, there was no telling how long the stalemate would last. And no matter how often Tamara reminded herself that Marcela was solely at fault, she couldn't help feeling guilty for being the cause of so much dissension.

Watching the play of emotions across her face, Victor pulled her gently into his arms and kissed the top of her head. "Don't worry, *cariño,*" he murmured. "Everything's gonna be just fine."

Tamara snuggled against his solid warmth, closed her eyes and silently prayed that he was right.

Chapter 16

"Are you ready?"

Tamara nodded quickly. "I'm ready."

"Are you sure?"

She sighed with impatience, tempted to pluck Victor's hand off her closed eyelids. "I'm ready. And I still don't understand why I have to be blindfolded. It's not as if I'm seeing the condo for the first—" She broke off with a startled squeak as he suddenly swept her off her feet and into his arms, then carried her through the front door.

He removed his hand from her face. "Okay, you can look now."

Tamara opened her eyes, then let out a shocked gasp. "Oh, my God!"

"Surprise!" Victor exclaimed.

Tamara's stunned gaze swept around the apartment, taking in the chocolate and cream suede sofa and love seat, elegant leather ottoman, and large plasma television.

Her incredulous gaze swung back to Victor. "Where did this new furniture come from? Did you enter us into that HGTV show *My First Place?*"

"No," Victor said, laughing as he carried her into the living room and sat down on the sofa, keeping her on his lap. Reaching toward an exotic floral arrangement that had been left on the ottoman, he plucked out a small envelope nestled among the fragrant flowers and passed it to Tamara.

She eyed him inquisitively. "What's this?"

"Just read it," he told her.

With mounting curiosity, Tamara opened the envelope and removed the card. As soon as she saw her mother's sleek, distinctive handwriting, her throat tightened.

My precious Tamara,
When you were growing up, I wasn't able to give you all the nice things you may have wanted. But you never once complained. You were, and are, the most extraordinary daughter any parent could ever wish for. I'm so proud of you and the wonderful things you have already accomplished. I'm also proud of the wise choices you've made. Being with Victor is one of them. He's an amazing young man, and I know the two of you will make each other happy. Congratulations on taking the next step in your relationship. Here's some new furniture

to help you and Victor celebrate your new be-
ginnings.
Love always,
Mom

By the time Tamara finished reading the note, her
vision was blurred with tears. Closing her eyes, she placed
the card over her heart and whispered, "Thank you, Ma."

Victor tenderly kissed her shoulder. "Now you know
why I was being so secretive. Your mom really wanted
to surprise both of us, but one of us had to be available to
have the furniture delivered to the apartment today."

Tamara gave him a watery smile. "It was a wonderful
surprise. You and Ma got me so good."

Victor grinned. "It wasn't easy to pull off. You ask too
many damn questions, woman."

"No, I don't." She hesitated, biting her lip. "But just
out of curiosity, where's *our* furniture?"

"See what I mean." Victor laughed, shaking his head
at her. "Our living room furniture has been donated to
the Salvation Army. Is that okay with you?"

"Absolutely," she said, sweeping an appreciative glance
around. The contemporary furnishings, combined with
the large picture windows, made the place look like something out of an interior design magazine.

A soft smile touched her lips. "Thank you, Ma," she
whispered again.

"Definitely," Victor agreed. "Your mom's an amazing
woman."

"She says the same thing about you." Tamara passed
the card to him, watching his expression soften as he read
Vonda's sentimental note.

"I really appreciate her support," he said quietly, and

Tamara knew he was thinking of his own mother, who remained adamantly opposed to their relationship.

Refusing to allow Marcela Aguilar's rejection to put a damper on their first night in their new place, Tamara pressed a tender kiss to Victor's forehead and smiled into his eyes. "Thank you for asking me to move in with you."

"Thank you for accepting." His lips twitched. "Eventually."

"Better late than never." She grinned. "And just to give you a heads-up, Jaclyn, Isabelle and Ravi have already invited themselves over for our housewarming party."

Victor chuckled. "Figures."

"I told them to give us a chance to get settled in first."

"Good," Victor said, his eyes glittering wickedly. "We need to christen every nook and cranny of this place."

Tamara gave him an amused look. "Somehow I don't think they'd want to know that."

"Hmm, probably not."

As Victor settled back against the sofa cushions, Tamara shifted until she was straddling his lap, her arms looped around his neck. "Before we left work, I ordered dinner from the gourmet delivery service," she told him. "Our meals should be here in twenty minutes. I ordered a lot of food, so I hope you're starving."

"Oh, I'm starving all right," Victor murmured, leaning forward to nibble her lips. "But not for food."

"That's too bad," Tamara purred against his mouth, "because food is all you're getting until later."

"Why wait until later," he drawled, running his hands under her skirt, "when we're both here now?"

"Because we shouldn't start something—" she shivered as his big, warm hands slipped beneath her silk panties and cupped her butt "—when we know we're going to be interrupted."

"I beg to differ," Victor countered, gently kneading her bottom. "See, the beauty of having our own place now is that we can always go back to what we were doing before we were interrupted."

"Is that so?"

"Absolutely."

Tamara eyed him suspiciously. "You know what I'm starting to think? I think—" Her breath caught sharply as he slipped a finger inside her.

"Yes?" His innocently inquisitive tone was belied by the gleam of wicked satisfaction in his eyes. "What do you think?"

"I think—" She closed her eyes, trembling as his finger reached deeper inside her while his thumb stroked the slick nub of her clitoris. She had to bite her lip hard to keep from moaning with pleasure.

"Poor baby," Victor said sympathetically. "You seem to be having trouble keeping your train of thought."

Opening her eyes, Tamara tried to glare at him, but failed miserably.

He grinned. "Say what's on your mind, sweetheart."

"I think you only asked me to move in with you—" she watched as he removed his finger from her body and slowly slid it into his mouth "—so you could have sex with me whenever you want."

"Mmm." He sucked his finger, his eyes closed in an expression of unadulterated ecstasy. Staring at him,

Tamara's nipples hardened and her belly quivered with arousal.

Slowly his lashes lifted, his smoky blue eyes locking onto hers. "Damn, you taste good. Now what were you saying?"

Tamara nearly swallowed her tongue. "Forget it."

"Are you sure?" he prodded silkily, unzipping his jeans. "Because it seemed awfully important a few moments ago."

Tamara shook her head distractedly, her mouth watering as she stared at his thick, engorged shaft. "It wasn't important."

"If you're sure…" His hands gripped her butt, lifting and positioning her over his jutting erection. As she took him into her body, they both groaned with mutual pleasure. Once she was settled fully astride him, they began moving together, their eyes locked onto each other's.

"You know you don't play fair," Tamara whispered.

His eyes glinted devilishly. "When did I ever say I would?"

"Hmm. Good point." She fell back in the support of his arms, moaning softly as his mouth latched on to the pulsing nerve at the hollow of her throat. He suckled her as she rocked up and down his granite-hard length, his hips arching to meet hers, stroke for powerful stroke.

They came together in a hot rush, shuddering and whispering each other's names. Tamara dropped her head weakly onto Victor's shoulder and buried her face against the side of his neck. He held her close, lazily running his hands up and down her back.

Seconds later the doorbell rang.

Tamara lifted her head from Victor's shoulder and stared at him.

A slow, irreverent grin curved his mouth. "Now *that's* what I call perfect timing."

Later that night, lying on his side with his head propped in his hand, Victor gazed down at Tamara's sleeping face. She lay snuggled against him, soft firelight dancing across her features, her dark, chestnut hair spilled across the thick blanket they'd spread over the floor hours earlier. A drowsy fire crackled in the hearth nearby, the hiss of flames and falling embers whispering through the air.

After enjoying a sumptuous gourmet meal, he and Tamara had carried their wineglasses into the living room and cuddled underneath a blanket to watch their brand-new plasma television. But after just a few minutes they'd ended up talking, picking up right where they'd left off over dinner. Victor marveled at the realization that Tamara was the first and only woman he'd ever met that he enjoyed conversing with as much as he enjoyed making love to. He and Tamara had so much in common, and they never seemed to run out of things to say to each other. Once they got into one of their deep conversations, it wasn't uncommon for them to look up and realize that three hours had passed.

Victor shared some of his favorite childhood memories from Colombia, describing traditions and pastimes he and his family had enjoyed before gang violence besieged their hometown. Tamara opened up to him about growing up without her father, telling him about the financial struggles she and her mother had faced, the storms they had weathered together. As Victor listened to her stories, he gained a deeper level of respect and admiration for mother and daughter, who were two of the strongest, most remarkable women he'd ever met.

Victor simply couldn't get enough of Tamara, whether they were baring their souls or taking each other to the heights of ecstasy. He was consumed with all things Tamara. Which was why, for the past half hour, he'd been suppressing the need to take a leak. He couldn't pull himself away from the lush warmth of Tamara's body, didn't want to take his eyes off her serenely beautiful face even for a moment.

Dios Mio, he thought with grim amusement. *You've got it bad, Aguilar.*

And that was putting it mildly.

Knowing he could no longer ignore the call of nature, Victor carefully rolled away from Tamara and got to his feet. After tugging on his pajama bottoms, he crept down the hall to the bathroom.

When he returned to the living room, he saw that Tamara had not stirred. Smiling softly, he turned and padded silently to the kitchen. Without turning on the light, he made his way to the refrigerator and opened the door, scanning the contents before grabbing a bottle of water.

As he drank, he ran through a mental checklist of things he had to do at the hospital, patients he needed to follow up on. Dr. Balmer had generously given him and Tamara the evening off to enjoy their first night at the condo. In flagrant disregard for the hospital's nonfraternization policy, she openly supported their relationship, telling them humorously, "As long as you don't endanger patients' lives because you're too busy daydreaming about each other, what you do in private is your business."

Chuckling softly at the memory, Victor took another deep swallow of water.

When the soft overhead light suddenly clicked on, he glanced toward the doorway. His pulse quickened at the sight of Tamara standing there, her hair tousled about her face and shoulders, the blanket wrapped around her nude body like a toga.

"Hey," Victor murmured. "Did I wake you?"

"Sort of." She hesitated, looking sheepish. "I missed your body heat."

He smiled. "Sorry."

"Don't be. It's not your fault I've already gotten so used to sleeping with you that I notice when you're gone."

His chest swelled. She had no idea how happy she'd just made him with that statement.

He watched as she came toward him, moving slowly so she wouldn't trip over the blanket. When she reached him, she snagged the bottled water from his hand and took a long, healthy swig.

Victor smiled indulgently. "You *do* know there's more in the fridge."

"Yup." Her dark eyes twinkled as she passed back the water. "But I like drinking your backwash."

"And I like drinking yours," Victor said, winking at her as he sipped from the bottle.

Tamara smiled, leaning back against the center island. "What were you just chuckling to yourself about?"

"I was thinking about what Dr. Balmer told us yesterday."

"About not endangering patients' lives while we're daydreaming about each other?"

"Yeah."

Tamara grinned. "That was pretty amusing. Not that there'd be anything remotely funny about overdosing our patients," she quickly clarified.

Victor grinned, leaning back against the counter and setting down the empty water bottle. "I know what you mean."

"Good." She chuckled ruefully, tucking her hair behind one ear. "I've never been a daydreamer."

"Neither have I."

"I'm too analytical—"

"—too grounded in reality. Task-oriented."

"Exactly," Tamara agreed, nodding emphatically. "And I've always been hyperaware of my surroundings—"

"Me, too. I've even been told that I have eyes in the back of my head."

Tamara laughed. "Me, too. So the idea of just tuning out everything and letting my mind wander into la-la land—"

"—seems crazy."

"Exactly." Tamara smiled. "So, yeah, I've never been a daydreamer."

"Me, neither."

Until I met you.

They stared at each other, the words hanging between them as clearly as if they'd been spoken.

After several moments, Tamara shook her head wonderingly at him. "We're really going to do this, aren't we?"

"Do what?"

"Live together. Have a relationship."

"Yeah," Victor said huskily, "we are."

She held his gaze another moment, then gave her head another shake. "It seems so surreal," she marveled, "when you consider how much we hated each other."

"'Hate' is such a strong word."

Tamara laughed. "Oh, I hated you. Trust me."

Smothering a grin, Victor said with sham innocence, "I don't know what I ever did to make you feel that way about me."

Tamara snorted. "Yeah, right! Need I remind you of the first day of our internship? Everyone was so nervous and jittery. Before the morning rounds, Dr. De Winter gathered us together to go over some logistical things. I asked him a question—I can't even remember what it was—but no sooner had the words left my mouth than I heard this…this *kissing* noise. Like someone was trying to imply that I was sucking up to Dr. De Winter. I looked over my shoulder and there you were, wearing the most infuriatingly cocky grin I'd ever seen. Everyone started laughing. I was so embarrassed, I wanted to reach back and punch you right in the face. Just thinking about it burns my boots. *Grrr.*"

Victor threw back his head and roared with laughter.

"It's not funny," Tamara muttered darkly. "I really wanted to kick your ass, Victor."

"I know," he said, wiping tears of mirth from the corners of his eyes, "and that's what makes it so funny. Because truth be told, I actually thought you were pretty hot the moment I saw you."

Tamara looked surprised. "Really?"

"Hell, yeah. I remember walking into the locker

room that day, and you were rushing to fix your ponytail. You flipped your hair forward, then back, and I was like, *'Dayuum.'*" He grinned, shaking his head at the memory. "Maybe what I did to you that morning was my juvenile way of getting your attention."

"Oh, you got it all right. After that day, you were at the top of my hit list. Every time I saw you, I felt homicidal." A small, playful grin tugged at her lips. "But maybe you can be forgiven if you were only trying to get my attention."

"Um…"

Her eyes narrowed. "So you really *were* trying to embarrass me?"

Victor grinned at her. "You *were* kind of a suck-up at the beginning."

"I was not!"

"Were, too."

"Was not."

"Okay."

They stared at each other, then burst out laughing.

"That was one of the shortest arguments we've ever had!" Tamara exclaimed.

"I know." Victor grinned. "Crazy, isn't it?"

"Very."

Sobering after several moments, Victor murmured, "I could get very used to this."

Tamara held his gaze. "I think I already have."

Victor's heart knocked against his rib cage.

Straightening slowly from the cabinet, he walked over to her. As she stared up at him, he framed her face between his hands and slanted his mouth over hers. Her lips parted at once, her silky tongue stealing out to slide against the seam of his lips. He groaned softly at the sensation, arousal tightening in his groin until it was an acute, throbbing ache.

He held her head as he ate at her mouth, licking and devouring her like he'd never get enough of her. And he didn't think he ever would. How could he when she tasted so hot and sweet, her mouth flavored with a unique nectar that was custom made to drive him out of his mind?

The blanket fell away from her body, then her arms were encircling his neck as he wrapped his hands around her waist and lifted her onto the center island. Her breath hitched as he settled his hips between her legs, rocking against her in a carnal, unmistakable rhythm. She moaned as her hands roamed over him, moving up and down his back, over his ass, drawing him closer until he could feel the wet, tantalizing heat of her sex against his abdomen.

Breaking the kiss, Tamara grasped his pajama bottoms and shoved them down his hips. When his heavy shaft sprang free, she curled her warm fingers around him, erotically stroking up and down until a trickle of precum seeped out of him. She swiped her thumb over the silky moisture and licked herself clean, moaning as if she'd just sampled the most scrumptious delicacy.

"Tamara," Victor groaned hoarsely. *"Te necesito."*

"I need you, too," she whispered.

Unable to wait another second—relieved that he didn't have to—Victor stepped out of his pants, then quickly pushed her legs apart and stood between them.

Their eyes locked as he thrust deep and hard, penetrating her as far as he could possibly go. Tamara mewled, a sound of wanton pleasure that fueled his voracious hunger. She tightened her thighs around his hips and planted her hands on the counter to anchor herself as he began plunging inside her with a heavy, pounding rhythm.

"Victor," she moaned, closing her eyes and licking her lips. "Ohh...baby..."

He lowered his head, his mouth latching on to the ripeness of a plump, chocolate-tipped breast. She cried out, throwing back her head as he fed on first one, then the other luscious mound.

As her hips undulated against him, he grasped her round butt cheeks and lifted her off the counter, pumping into her until she arched backward with a breathless cry. As her body convulsed with spasms, he kept thrusting, pounding her juicy insides until he couldn't take any more. His head went back, eyes squeezing shut as he came with a force that wrenched an exultant shout from his throat.

He didn't know how long they remained locked together, Tamara's slick thighs wrapped around him, neither willing to end the intimate embrace.

As their breathing gradually returned to normal, Victor gently set her down on the countertop and trailed a line of kisses from her forehead to her softly parted lips.

"Te adoro," he whispered huskily, the words of love pouring out of him. *"No puedo vivir sin ti. Quiero estar contigo para siempre."* He kissed her closed eyelids. *"Te amo."*

Her lashes lifted as she opened her eyes to meet his fiercely tender gaze. *"Te amo,"* she repeated with soft wonder. "Did you just say...?"

Victor nodded vigorously. "I love you, Tamara. I love you so damn much."

Tears swam into her eyes. "I love you, too, baby."

His heart turned over. *"¿Te casarás conmigo?"*

She eyed him almost frantically. "English, Victor. *English.*"

"Sorry. I got carried away." He smiled. "Will you marry me?"

"What?" she whispered, staring at him in shock.

"I love you. I want to spend the rest of my life with you. So will you be my wife?"

"Oh, my God," she breathed, shaking her head at him. "You can't do this to me."

"Do what to you?"

"You can't propose to me, Victor. Not now. It's too soon. Everything's happening too fast."

This wasn't going the way he'd hoped. "So is that a no?"

"Yes. I mean, *no.* I mean—" Flustered, she cupped a trembling hand to her mouth and stared at him with wide, conflicted eyes.

"Listen," Victor said gently, "I'm not trying to rush you into anything you're not ready for. Maybe it *was* too soon for me to propose. But I love you, Tamara, and my feelings aren't going to change."

"I love you, too, Victor. And I've known that for a while. But I'm scared," she admitted tearfully. "And with everything that's happening with your mother, it just feels like there's a dark cloud hanging over our relationship."

As tears streamed down her face, Victor tenderly wiped them away with his thumb. "Don't cry, *cariño,*" he murmured soothingly. "I understand your fears and reservations, and I'm not going to pressure you into giving me an answer tonight. But you need to know that I'm not going anywhere. If the whole world turns against us tomorrow, you'll still have my love. Do you believe me?"

She hesitated, then nodded slowly.

"Good." He kissed her softly on the mouth, then swept her into his arms and strode from the kitchen with such focused determination, Tamara asked teasingly, "Where's the fire?"

He slanted her a wolfish grin. "The night is still young, and we've got several more areas to christen."

She groaned playfully. "I knew I should have stayed asleep."

"Too late now, sweetheart. Too late now."

Chapter 17

Three days later, Tamara was awakened from a deep slumber by the peal of the doorbell. Groaning in protest, she rolled over in the large, rumpled bed and squinted at the alarm clock. It was just after 1:00 p.m. She'd worked a double shift yesterday and had been hoping to catch up on her rest while Victor was gone, since the man's voracious sexual appetite was impervious to such pesky things as sleep deprivation.

He'd left that morning to sit in on a lobectomy for an eighty-year-old patient with stage three lung cancer. Victor had bonded with the Vietnam veteran, listening to the old man's war stories and memorizing the names and ages of his ten grandchildren. Last night in bed, he and Tamara had stayed up late discussing Tobias Clemmons's deteriorating condition and grim prognosis. Although they'd both tried to remain optimistic throughout the conversation, Tamara knew there was a very strong chance that Mr. Clemmons would not survive the surgery.

Before Victor left for the hospital that morning, Tamara had taken his hands between hers and prayed quietly with him, asking that God's will be done. When Victor lifted his head and met her gaze, his eyes had been bright with unshed tears. If there'd been any doubt in Tamara's mind that she loved him, that moment would have sealed the deal for her.

Although she was on call that day, she sincerely hoped she wouldn't get paged. She wanted to prepare a special, romantic dinner for Victor to help bolster his spirits in case the surgery didn't go well.

The doorbell rang again, pulling her out of her reverie.

Filling her lungs with the clean, masculine scent that clung to Victor's pillow, Tamara dragged herself out of bed, tugged on her pajama bottoms and padded from the sun-drenched room.

When she opened the front door, she was stunned to find Marcela Aguilar standing there with an armful of groceries. As if she hadn't been punishing Tamara and Victor with her silence for the past two weeks. As if she wasn't responsible for casting a pall over their relationship.

Recovering her composure, Tamara said coldly, "Victor's not here."

"I know," Marcela said quietly. "I came to see you."

Surprised, Tamara stared at her.

"May I come in?"

Tamara hesitated for a long moment, then nodded and opened the door wider.

As Marcela entered the condo, she swept an appreciative glance around. "My sons were right. Your home is very lovely."

"Thank you," Tamara murmured.

Since she and Victor had been unable to get time off from work, he'd enlisted his younger brothers to help with the move. Thanks to the hard work of Alejandro, Christian, Fernando and Roberto, Tamara hadn't needed to lift a finger. To show their appreciation, she and Victor had treated the boys to dinner and got them tickets to a Washington Redskins game. Tamara had hit it off so well with the four rowdy siblings that she looked forward to getting to know them better.

Their mother, on the other hand, was a different story.

"Let me help you with those bags," Tamara offered, taking the load from Marcela and heading toward the kitchen.

Marcela followed her. "What a beautiful kitchen," she exclaimed, admiring the ultramodern finishes and stainless steel appliances. She walked over to the gleaming refrigerator and pulled both doors open, peering inside. "This isn't quite as big as the one Victor bought for me last year."

Setting the grocery bags down on the center island, Tamara eyed the refrigerator, which was considerably larger than any she'd ever owned. "He must have bought you a Sub-Zero."

"Yes." Marcela smiled. "It's very roomy. I can fit everything in there."

"Which is no small feat," Tamara said wryly, "considering how large your family is."

Marcela's smile widened. "Exactly."

It was the first friendly exchange they'd ever had.

Nervously tucking her hair behind one ear, Tamara nodded toward the brown paper bags on the counter. "It was kind of you to bring us groceries, Mrs. Aguilar, but we really don't need anything."

"Oh, those aren't groceries. They're ingredients for *Bandeja Paisa.*"

"Bandeja Paisa?"

"Sí. It's a traditional Colombian meal served with grilled steak, fried pork, chorizo sausage, red beans and white rice, and topped with avocado and fried bananas."

"Sounds delicious," Tamara said. "Fattening, but delicious."

"It's one of Victor's favorite dishes, so I thought I would teach you how to make it." Marcela hesitated uncertainly. "If you'd like."

Recognizing that she'd just been extended an olive branch, Tamara smiled softly. "I'd like that very much."

Marcela's smile was tinged with relief. "Good."

"Can I offer you something to drink, Mrs. Aguilar? Some coffee or tea? Maybe a glass of wine, if it's not too early for you?"

The woman hesitated. "Wine would be nice."

"Do you prefer a red or a white?"

"Doesn't matter." She smiled at Tamara. "I'll let you choose."

"All right." Tamara walked to the butler's pantry and removed a pinot noir from the wine rack. As she uncorked the bottle and retrieved glasses, Marcela sat down on one of the bar stools at the center island and folded her hands on the countertop as she watched Tamara.

Her silent scrutiny made Tamara feel self-conscious. Even after she returned to the island and handed Marcela her drink, the woman continued observing her.

Shifting uncomfortably from one bare foot to the other, Tamara asked, "Is something wrong?"

"No." Marcela smiled softly. "I didn't mean to stare at you. You're a very beautiful girl, Tamara. I can see why my son couldn't resist you."

"Um…" Tamara didn't know whether to be flattered or offended. Was the woman suggesting that Tamara had used her looks to ensnare Victor? Was she saying that her son's interest was purely physical in nature?

Marcela chuckled, correctly interpreting her thoughts. "Don't worry, *mija*. It was a compliment."

"Oh." Tamara bit her lip. "In that case, thank you."

"You're welcome." Marcela took a sip of her wine. "Mmm. That's good."

"Think so? Victor says it's too sweet."

"Victor's like his father. He prefers beer over wine."

"I'll have to remember that." Tamara lowered herself onto a stool across from her guest and gave her a small, lazy grin. "What was he like as a child?"

Marcela sighed. "Victor was very playful and mischievous. A prankster."

Tamara's grin turned wry. "Why doesn't that surprise me?"

"Ah, but he could also be very intense. Curious." A nostalgic smile curved Marcela's mouth. "If he came across a dead animal in the street—a bird, a frog, a cat—he'd want to know exactly how and why it had died." She laughed, laying a hand over her heart. "He once brought home a dead rattlesnake. Ran right into the kitchen yelling excitedly, *'Mira, mira, Mama!'*

When I turned around and saw that big snake in his hands, I nearly had a heart attack!"

Tamara laughed. "I can imagine."

Marcela grinned. "He wanted to cut it open and study its intestines. I screamed at him, telling him if he didn't get that thing out of my house, I'd ship him off to an orphanage. And do you know what that boy said? He looked up at me with those innocent blue eyes and asked me if the orphanage would allow him to keep a pet snake."

The two women shared a long, gusty laugh.

Sobering several moments later, Marcela took another sip of her wine, then carefully set down the glass and pinned Tamara with an unflinchingly direct gaze. "I'm sorry for the way I spoke to you at dinner that night."

Tamara was silent, caught off guard by the apology.

"I'm ashamed of my behavior," Marcela continued grimly, "although it took me a while to realize that I should be."

Tamara met her gaze. "Why do you have a problem with your son dating a black woman?"

Marcela sighed heavily. "I've always told myself that there's nothing wrong with wanting my children to stick with their own kind. That's how most people are in any culture. I work with a Chinese woman whose children are only allowed to marry other Chinese people. Another coworker of mine won't hear of her daughter marrying anyone but a black man, preferably one who graduated from an HC...HB—"

"HBCU," Tamara supplied. "Historically black colleges and universities."

"Yes. That's her preference. So you see, I never thought there was anything wrong with me having requirements for my own sons, because that's just the way it was." Marcela paused, choosing her next words carefully. "I didn't grow up around many Afro-Colombians. My father didn't…well, he didn't trust them. He thought they were dishonest and lazy. So my siblings and I weren't allowed to associate with the few that we knew."

"I see," Tamara said coolly.

Marcela stared into the twinkling ruby contents of her glass. "I didn't realize how much I held some of my father's racist views about black people until I met you, Tamara. You called me out that night. And even though it was, as they say, a bitter pill to swallow, I'm glad you did. I needed to look in the mirror and examine myself. And when I did, I wasn't very pleased with what I saw."

Tamara said nothing. She knew how difficult it was for such a proud woman to admit that she was wrong, so she respected Marcela's honesty and courage.

"Victor's brothers told me they've never seen him so happy," Marcela said quietly, meeting Tamara's gaze. "Alejandro said when you and Victor look at each other, it's like you're in your own private world. And I saw that with my own two eyes that night."

Tamara held her gaze. "I love Victor very much, Mrs. Aguilar."

"I know." Reaching across the counter, Marcela gently took her hand. "You make my son happy, Tamara. As far as I'm concerned, that makes you absolutely perfect for him."

Tamara's throat tightened with emotion. "Thank you," she whispered.

Marcela smiled softly. "Thank *you.*"

Victor was exhausted when he returned home later that afternoon—exhausted and demoralized. Despite everyone's best efforts, Tobias Clemmons had died on the operating table after suffering a collapsed lung during surgery. Though the old man wasn't the first patient Victor had lost, and he wouldn't be the last, Victor doubted he'd ever get used to telling family members that they'd never see their loved one alive again.

When he entered the condo, the first thing he noticed was the appetizing aroma of *Bandeja Paisa,* his favorite Colombian meal. At first he thought he was only imagining it. After the emotionally trying day he'd had, he could be craving some comfort food bad enough to conjure it out of thin air.

But no, Victor realized as he advanced into the apartment. The hot, spicy scent filling his nostrils was all too real, as were the sounds of feminine laughter wafting from the kitchen.

Intrigued, Victor dropped his helmet and duffel bag on the floor and followed his nose—and ears—across the room.

He froze in the kitchen doorway, unprepared for the sight that greeted him.

Tamara and his mother were busy making tortillas, or at least Marcela was. Tamara's hair was pulled back in its usual ponytail, the short, curly bits in the front forming a halo around her face. Her hands—those slender, beautiful hands that were learning to handle a scalpel with remarkable precision—were adorably clumsy as she patted the dough, trying valiantly to make her tortilla look like Marcela's. But when it came out more triangular than round, she threw back her head and laughed—that sweet, rollicking sound that always made Victor feel like he'd been visited by a naughty angel. His mother was laughing, too, clearly charmed by Tamara's infectious good humor.

When Tamara glanced over and saw Victor standing in the doorway, she beamed with such pleasure his chest ached. God, how he loved her.

"Hey, baby," she called out cheerfully. "We're making tortillas."

He smiled indulgently. "I see that."

When he met his mother's gaze, a silent look of understanding passed between them.

"I'm teaching Tamara how to make tortillas like my mother taught me." Marcela smiled meaningfully. "Maybe one day she can do the same for your daughter."

Victor's heart lodged in his throat.

Without a word, he walked over to Tamara and his mother, draped an arm around their shoulders and tenderly kissed each woman on the cheek.

Although he'd lost a patient that day, he suddenly felt like the luckiest man in the world.

Chapter 18

Over the next two weeks, Tamara and Victor happily settled into their new lives as roommates.

Although Tamara had initially claimed to want her own bedroom, she'd never had any intention of sleeping apart from Victor. So they'd gone shopping for a new king-size bed, and when it was delivered, they'd thoroughly enjoyed christening every square inch.

Living with Victor allowed Tamara to discover all facets of his personality, including the boyishly playful side, who stood on their private terrace every morning, let out a primal wail and thumped his chest like Tarzan.

Late one afternoon, Tamara returned home from her mother's house to find Victor swigging a beer and cooking steaks on the stove as one of his favorite tunes—"Rebelión" by Afro-Colombian artist Joe

Arroyo—blasted from the stereo. Grinning from ear to ear, Tamara had stood in the doorway watching as he belted out the Spanish lyrics while moving his hips in time to the catchy, salsa-infused song.

When she sashayed her way into the kitchen, he'd glanced up at her with a delighted grin. Setting down his spatula and beer, he'd taken her into his arms and led her into an improvised salsa dance. Tamara had matched his rhythm and step, sensually swiveling her hips and laughing as he twirled her around. They'd gotten so caught up in the fun, playful moment that the steaks nearly burned.

They enjoyed romantic candlelight dinners on their terrace, which boasted such a stunning view of the Potomac River that they could have been dining at a fancy waterfront restaurant.

Over the course of those two weeks, they became each other's sounding board, spending hours talking about their patients and seeking each other's advice. Tamara was ecstatic when the chief of surgery, Dr. Thomas Bradshaw, chose her to scrub in on a three-part surgery consisting of a double coronary artery bypass, an aortic valve replacement and the repair of an ascending aorta. Her excitement over being selected was tempered by fears that Victor would resent her for receiving such an amazing opportunity over him.

But she needn't have worried.

When she shared her great news with Victor, he was genuinely thrilled for her, taking her out to dinner to celebrate. On the day of the surgery, he and several other interns gathered in the viewing gallery to watch the dramatic operation. At one point, Tamara lifted her head and looked right at Victor. Eyes glowing with pride and adoration, he smiled and gave her a thumbs up.

And Tamara fell harder in love.

Late one night, they were lying on a blanket in front of a cozy fire, sated from hours of lovemaking and lulled by the soothing lash of rain against the living room windows.

Idly running her fingers through Victor's thick, silky hair, Tamara murmured, "Do you know when I first realized that I loved you?"

Victor had been lying on his stomach with his head resting on his arms, his eyes closed as he luxuriated in her gentle caress. Hearing Tamara's question, he slowly opened his eyes to meet her tender gaze.

"When did you realize?" he asked softly.

She smiled. "It was the day I walked into Bethany Dennison's room and saw you arm wrestling her kid brother."

A flicker of surprise crossed Victor's face. "The same day I asked you out on a date?"

She nodded. "I didn't admit it to myself then, because I was still in denial about the way everything had changed between us. But seeing you with little Decker... It melted my heart, Victor."

He eyed her wonderingly. "I had no idea."

"You weren't supposed to. I was in denial, remember?" She smiled softly. "I didn't admit it to myself until the night we had dinner with your parents. Afterward, when I was at my mother's house and we were rehashing everything that had happened, she told me that you and I clearly loved each other. And that's when

I finally admitted—to myself and out loud—that, yes, I had fallen in love with you."

Victor's expression softened. He reached out, gently stroking her cheek. "Your mother is very perceptive if she realized how we felt about each other after just an hour in our company." His gaze roamed across her face. "Truth be told, I've probably been in love with you since the night we got stranded at the hospital."

Surprised, Tamara stared at him. "Really?"

He nodded. "We connected in a way I never thought was possible. I couldn't stop thinking about you after that night."

"And I couldn't stop thinking about you," Tamara confessed.

"If I hadn't already been a goner, hearing about how you went to bat for me with Dudley would have done the trick."

Tamara smiled ruefully. "Not that I think it made any difference—"

"It made all the difference in the world to me," Victor said huskily. "So nothing else matters."

Tamara turned her face into his palm and tenderly kissed it. "I'm so lucky to have you in my life," she whispered.

He held her gaze. "I think *I'm* the lucky one."

"We're both lucky. How about that?"

He chuckled softly. "Sounds like a good compromise."

Tamara grinned. Imitating his pose, she rested her head on her arms and stared at him, watching as soft firelight danced across his face, a face she'd never grow tired of looking at.

Since their first night in the condo, Victor hadn't

broached the subject of marriage again, even though the rift with his mother—Tamara's main reason for turning down his proposal—was no longer an issue. He'd promised not to pressure her, and he was keeping that promise. Yet Tamara found herself wondering whether he'd changed his mind about wanting to marry her. Although she still wasn't ready to give him an answer, she needed to know that she hadn't forfeited her one and only chance to become Mrs. Victor Aguilar.

Striving for a casual tone, she asked, "Since your family is Catholic, does that mean you'd be expected to get married in a Catholic church?"

Victor went still, searching her face. "More than likely." He paused. "Do you think that would be a problem?"

"It could be," Tamara said carefully, "if your bride was raised a Baptist, and her pastor had always looked forward to officiating her wedding. Hypothetically speaking, of course."

"Of course." Victor slowly propped himself up on one elbow. "As the groom, I'd be willing to make some compromises. Especially if it seemed that the location of the ceremony meant more to my bride than it did to me." He paused. "Hypothetically speaking, of course."

"Of course," Tamara said with mock sobriety.

"So…do you think my bride would have any special locations in mind for the reception? Preferably someplace big enough to accommodate my large family and every Colombian my parents know."

Smothering a laugh, Tamara replied neutrally, "Now that you mention it, there's a historic mansion not far from here that would make the perfect venue for a romantic wedding reception. Waterfront views, landscaped grounds, beautiful gardens. I'm sure you and your bride, as well as your guests, would be very pleased."

"Oh, I'm sure," Victor agreed with an irrepressible grin. "And since you're on a roll, where do you think my bride would want to go on our honeymoon?"

"Well, speaking for *myself,* I've always thought Italy made a perfect honeymoon destination." Tamara sighed. "But I'm sure you and your bride could reach a consensus that you're both happy with."

"Oh, of course," Victor said with exaggerated earnestness. "After all, the most important thing is that we'd be together, and looking forward to spending the rest of our lives together."

"Of course." Tamara smiled at him.

He smiled back, his eyes gleaming in the firelight.

"Well." He sat up abruptly and rolled to his feet. "Thanks for the information. You've been most helpful."

Mouth agape, Tamara watched as he sauntered, unabashedly naked, from the room. "Where are you going?"

"To bed. *One* of us has to be up early."

"But we're not finished—"

"Good night, Tamara."

Sputtering with mock indignation, she jumped up and chased after him. He laughed as she hopped onto his back, arms looping around his neck, legs wrapping around his waist.

"I don't think my bride would take too kindly to me having a naked woman on my back," he drawled.

Tamara grinned, nipping his ear. "What she doesn't know won't hurt her...."

Chapter 19

Three days later, Tamara stood at the bedside of a critically ill patient who needed a new intravenous tube. She was just about to unwrap a sterile needle when Sheryl Newsome bustled into the room.

"I'll take care of this, hon," the nurse said briskly to Tamara.

"Oh, that's okay, Sheryl. I can—"

Without warning, Sheryl grabbed her shoulders, urgently turning her around. The gentle concern in the woman's green eyes sent a dagger of alarm through Tamara. "Your mother was just brought into the E.R. There was an accident—"

She'd barely finished before Tamara was racing out of the room, panic and fear choking the air from her lungs as she rushed downstairs to the emergency room.

She ran past a blur of concerned faces, shrugging off

hands that reached out to detain her. "Where is she?" she shouted hoarsely, charging through the bustling triage area. *"Where's my mother?"*

That was when she saw Dr. Balmer, Victor and several other physicians working frantically on the unconscious body of a woman on a stretcher.

The blood drained from Tamara's head.

"Mama!" she screamed, rushing over and shoving her way through the figures huddled around the stretcher.

Vonda lay with an oxygen mask over her face, which was covered with blood and multiple lacerations—an image straight out of Tamara's worst nightmare.

As the ground swayed beneath her feet, Victor turned and caught her, holding her upright. "Get her out of here!" he yelled to an EMT, who snapped to attention and hustled over.

"I'm not going anywhere!" Tamara cried, jerking out of the man's grasp. "I want to see my mother!"

"Listen to me," Victor said with fierce urgency, all but carrying Tamara away from the stretcher. "You're in no shape to be here right now. Let us get her stabilized—"

"Why didn't anyone page me?" Tamara demanded hysterically. *"Why didn't anyone page me?!"*

"I told them to wait."

"How dare you? She's my—"

"Blood pressure's sixty over thirty!" Dr. Balmer called out warningly.

When Tamara lunged forward in alarm, Victor grabbed her. Though she struggled to break free, he held fast, his blue eyes locking on to hers like a laser beam.

"You can't be here, baby. You know how this works. You need to go to the waiting room."

"She's my mother!"

"And now she's a patient," Victor growled, swiftly transitioning from concerned lover to a doctor who had a job to do. "She's lost a lot of blood, so we need to get her to the O.R. As soon as she's been prepped for surgery, I'll come talk to you. I promise."

"Victor—" Tamara whimpered.

"I promise." He grabbed her face between his hands and pressed a hard kiss to her mouth, then nodded tersely to the EMT, who'd been joined by a second one. The two men stepped forward and gently but firmly escorted Tamara away.

She spent the next forty minutes frantically pacing back and forth in the empty waiting room. She'd spoken to the police officer who'd been the first to arrive at the scene of her mother's car accident. According to his explanation, Vonda had been traveling down Route One—no doubt on her way to the hospital to surprise Tamara—when she collided with another driver, who'd apparently lost control of his vehicle on the rain-slicked road. The officer's repeated assurances that the other motorist was at fault had brought Tamara no consolation, nor was she comforted by the news that the other driver had escaped the collision with only minor injuries.

Nothing would console Tamara if her mother didn't survive.

She was on the verge of falling apart when Victor finally appeared, his dark hair concealed beneath the blue, red and yellow scrub cap that paid homage to Co-lombia's national soccer team.

Tamara swooped down on him. "How is she? How are her vitals? Was Dr. Balmer able to get her stabilized? What—"

"Come on. Sit down." Taking her clammy hands between his, Victor backed her into a chair, then crouched down to bring himself to eye level with her. His expression was grim. "Your mother sustained internal bleeding from the collision. Dr. Balmer's primary concern is making sure she doesn't bleed out—"

Tamara gasped, tears rushing to her eyes. "Oh, my God," she whispered brokenly. "This can't be happening. *Oh, God...*"

"Listen to me." Victor cupped her cheek in his hand, his eyes tunneling into hers. "I need you to stay calm for me. I know that's easier said than done under the circumstances, but we're racing against the clock here. So I need you to think like a doctor right now, not like a daughter who's rightfully terrified of losing her mother. Can you do that for me?"

Tamara nodded weakly. "What happens now, Victor?"

"I suggested freezing your mother's body."

"What?"

"Let me explain. It's a radical new technique I've read up on. It's called emergency preservation resuscitation, where surgeons induce extreme hypothermia in trauma patients to give themselves more time to protect the patient's brain and other vital organs from damage."

"I've heard of the procedure," Tamara said sickly. "It's been done on animals, and similar techniques have been used on heart patients and stroke victims. But even in those rare cases, the patients were treated with mild induced hypothermia. What *you're* proposing is to drop my mother's body temperature down to—"

"Between ten and fifteen degrees Celsius."

"What!" Tamara stared at him, aghast. "She'd be clinically dead, Victor!"

"Technically." He paused, his mouth set in a grim line. "It's a risky technique, but that risk has to be balanced against the very real threat of your mother hemorrhaging to death. The surgery she needs is going to put her in more jeopardy. Freezing her body will buy Dr. Balmer more time—up to three hours—to work on her."

Tamara anxiously searched his face. "How would it be done? How exactly does the procedure work?"

"The key is that her body has to be cooled rapidly," he explained. "In order to do this, a pump will be connected to the major blood vessels around her heart to remove the warm blood and replace it with a cold saline solution."

Tamara eyed him incredulously, then shot to her feet and began pacing up and down the floor. "You're basically telling me that you want to take my mother to the brink of death, and then try to bring her back."

Victor dropped his head for a moment, then said with grave solemnity, "Your mother's already in critical condition, Tamara. The reality is that she may not even survive surgery."

Tamara clamped her hand over her mouth, but the anguished sob escaped anyway. Collapsing into the nearest chair, she leaned her head back against the wall and closed her eyes as the room spun sickeningly around her.

Victor walked over and sat down beside her, gently folding her into his arms. As she buried her face against his chest and began sobbing, he stroked her back and whispered soothingly to her.

"I know you're terrified of making the wrong decision," he said quietly. "But in my medical opinion, inducing extreme hypothermia is your mother's best chance for survival right now."

Tamara remembered the argument they'd had over prescribing Naphtomycin to Mrs. Gruener. When Tamara insisted that the drug was unproven and therefore too dangerous to administer, Victor had challenged her to ask herself what she would do if Mrs. Gruener were her mother. *Until you're in that situation,* he'd told her, *you have no idea what measures you'd take to help your mother.*

How eerily prescient those words had been.

Opening her eyes, she lifted her head and found Victor watching her intently. She could feel his body thrumming with tension and adrenaline.

"We don't have a lot of time here, Tamara. Dr. Balmer's waiting for your consent before she proceeds with the operation."

Tamara pulled out of his arms and shoved a trembling hand through her hair, paralyzed with terror and indecision. If she allowed Dr. Balmer to perform this radical procedure and her mother died, she'd never forgive Victor. But if her mother died because Tamara had been unwilling to take a necessary risk to save her, she'd never forgive *herself.*

"The night we got stranded at the hospital during the storm," Victor said in a low voice, "you told me that you wouldn't entrust your life to anyone but me. Did you mean that?"

Tamara nodded. "Yes," she whispered.

"Well, I'm asking you to trust my judgment, and allow Dr. Balmer to freeze your mother's body to give her a fighting chance." His eyes probed hers. "Can you do that, Tamara?"

She stared at him for an interminable moment. He'd been right about administering Naphtomycin to Mrs. Gruener. At last check, the woman's sternal wound seemed to be healing remarkably well.

Did Tamara dare take a gamble on trusting his judgment when the personal stakes were so much higher?

"Tamara?" Victor prompted, his voice laced with urgency.

She hesitated another moment, then swallowed hard and gave a shaky nod. "Okay," she whispered. "Do it. Save my mother."

Victor touched her face briefly, then rose and strode purposefully from the waiting room.

Left alone, Tamara drew her legs up to her chest and dropped her head onto her knees. As a fresh wave of tears spilled from her eyes, she told herself that she'd made the right decision.

God help her if she was wrong.

The next seven hours were the longest, most excruciating seven hours of Tamara's life.

She paced restlessly, wept frequently and petitioned God for a miracle. Isabelle, Ravi, Jaclyn and Dr. De Winter took turns sitting and talking with her, assuring her that her mother was in excellent hands. Sheryl and Jerome Stubbs brought Tamara something to eat and wouldn't leave until she'd forced down a few bites. Even Dr. Dudley and Nurse Tsang came by to check up on her and offer kind words of comfort.

As much as Tamara appreciated the moral support of her concerned colleagues and friends, she couldn't draw an easy breath as long as her mother's life hung in the balance. Vonda St. John meant everything to her. She was Tamara's best friend and confidant, her Rock of Gibraltar. Tamara couldn't imagine a world without her mother in it. Losing her would be a devastating tragedy she would never, ever recover from.

Finally, after an agonizing eternity, Victor and Dr. Balmer returned to the waiting room to deliver the news of her mother's fate. By then, Tamara was surrounded by nearly everyone who had visited her throughout the day, including several of her mother's friends and co-workers who'd rushed over as soon as they heard about the accident.

The appearance of Victor and Dr. Balmer brought the roomful of people to their feet, an expectant hush sweeping over them.

Victor and Dr. Balmer scanned the faces in the crowd before their gazes came to rest on Tamara.

She held her breath, heart slamming painfully against her ribcage.

Slow, satisfied smiles swept across the doctors' faces. "The operation was a success," Dr. Balmer announced.

As the room erupted into cheers, Tamara, bursting with elation and gratitude, rushed forward to embrace her supervisor.

"Thank you," she said fervently. "Thank you for saving my mother's life!"

"You're welcome, Tamara," Dr. Balmer said warmly. "But I really can't take all the credit. Victor's the one who recommended inducing extreme hypothermia. Without his gutsy suggestion, we could have been dealing with an entirely different outcome right now."

Beaming with excitement, Tamara turned and leaped into Victor's arms. He laughed, lifting her off the floor and twirling her around as she showered his face with grateful kisses.

"Thank you *so* much, Victor!"

He grinned. "Haven't I told you what an amazing woman your mother is?"

"Yes! Can I go see her?"

"Absolutely," he said.

As Dr. Balmer remained behind to accept more congratulations, Tamara and Victor made their way quickly to the Intensive Care Unit.

Tamara took one look at her mother lying in the metal hospital bed—bandaged and bruised, but very much alive—and broke down in tears. Before she could compose herself, she was hurrying to Vonda's bedside and leaning down to kiss her cheek and hug her warm body, thoroughly shaken by how close she'd come to losing her.

Vonda stirred, her eyes opening to settle groggily on Tamara's tear-streaked face. "Hey, baby," she murmured.

"Hey, yourself." Tamara managed a tremulous smile as she reluctantly pulled away, gently stroking her mother's hair. "You gave me quite a scare today, didn't you?"

Vonda sighed. "I suppose I did. Certainly didn't mean to."

"I know." Tamara sniffled as she perched on the side of the bed, resisting the urge to curl up beside her mother and remain there until Vonda was discharged from the hospital. "How are you feeling, Ma?"

"Honestly? Like I'm on some psychedelic mind trip."

Tamara gave a watery grin. "It's the anesthesia. It'll wear off soon."

"Mmm." Staring beyond her daughter's shoulder, Vonda smiled warmly at Victor, who'd remained near the doorway to give mother and daughter some privacy. "Ah, there he is. There's the man who helped save my life. But why are you standing all the way over there?"

Victor chuckled, walking slowly to the bed. "You've spent the past seven hours around me. I figured you needed a break."

Vonda gave a soft laugh.

"That sound is music to my ears," Tamara and Victor told her, then looked at each other and grinned.

Catching the affectionate exchange, Vonda smiled with quiet satisfaction before saying, "I overheard the nurses talking excitedly when they brought me to my room. Is it true that you suggested freezing me like a Popsicle, Victor?"

He laughed. "Something like that."

Vonda's smile widened. "Guess I'll have quite a story to share when I go back to work."

"You certainly will," Victor agreed, gently touching her face.

"And speaking of your coworkers, Ma," Tamara added, "a bunch of them showed up at the hospital this afternoon. They're in the waiting room, hoping they'll get a chance to see you. But I don't want you to overexert yourself, so I'll tell them to come back tomorrow."

"That's fine. This anesthesia's got me feeling a little too loopy for visitors, anyway." Vonda divided a glance between Tamara and Victor, a hazy smile curving her lips. "I had a dream about the two of you."

Tamara and Victor exchanged looks.

"What was the dream about, Ma?" Tamara asked.

Vonda sighed contentedly. "It was wonderful. You were married, and you had beautiful twins. A boy and a girl who took after each of you."

Tamara and Victor shared another long, meaningful glance.

By the time their gazes returned to Vonda, her eyes had drifted closed.

Tamara leaned forward, tenderly kissing her mother's cheek. "Get some rest, Ma. Victor and I will check up on you later."

Vonda didn't respond. She had fallen asleep.

As Tamara carefully rose from the bed, Victor took her hand in his, caressing her palm with his fingers.

They were halfway across the room when Vonda's soft, drowsy voice floated out to them. "Or maybe it wasn't a dream. Maybe it was a vision of the future." She sighed. "Either way, it gave me even more of a reason to pull through...."

Chapter 20

Over the next several days, Tamara remained a constant fixture at her mother's bedside, thanks to the time off that Dr. Balmer had generously allotted her. Victor also stopped by frequently to check on his patient, pleased by how well she was recovering from the risky operation that had made her an instant celebrity around the hospital.

Although Tamara wanted to spend every night in her mother's room to keep a close eye on her, Vonda wouldn't hear of it. She shooed Tamara out at the end of each day, telling her to go home to Victor where she belonged.

On her way back to the condo one evening, Tamara reflected on her mother's admonition, and her use of the word *home*. Before moving in together, Tamara and Victor had regarded their apartments as places to lay their heads, and nothing more. But the condo they now shared meant more to them than either could have ever imagined. They'd built a home together—one where they laughed and frolicked together, played music and danced together, cooked and ate together, made love and created sweet, lasting memories together.

As Tamara drove home that night, she remembered what Victor had told her that day in the supply closet when he'd held his stethoscope to her chest. When she'd asked him what he was doing, he'd replied, *Listening to your heart. You should try it sometime.*

She'd never forgotten those words. She'd been afraid to trust her feelings for Victor. She'd been afraid to trust her heart. But no longer. Nearly losing her mother had reminded her of just how precious life was. Love, too, was a precious gift that should never be taken for granted.

So when Tamara returned home from the hospital that evening to find Victor napping on the sofa, she set down her backpack, toed off her shoes and crept over to the living room. As she climbed on top of Victor and straddled his legs, he opened his eyes and stared at her.

"Hey," he greeted her softly. "How's your mom doing?"

"Wonderful. But as much as she's been enjoying the VIP treatment, she's looking forward to going home tomorrow. Even when I invited her to stay here with us until she's fully recuperated, she politely refused. She wants her own space again."

Victor chuckled. "That's understandable. We're both doctors, and even *we* sometimes feel caged in at the hospital."

"True." Tamara leaned down and kissed him, a long, deep, passionate kiss that left them both breathless.

"Wow," Victor murmured, stroking her thighs. "What was that for?"

"My answer's yes."

His hands stilled. "Yes to…?"

"Yes, Victor, I'll marry you."

He stared at her, searching her face as if he couldn't quite believe what he'd heard. "Did you just say…"

"Yes, sweetheart. I want to be your wife and spend the rest of my life with you. And the sooner, the better."

Whooping with triumphant elation, Victor sank his hands into her hair and crushed his mouth to hers.

Long moments later when they drew apart, both wore huge, delighted grins.

"We should call our parents," Tamara said breathlessly. "They'll want to know our good news as soon as possible."

"We can call them later," Victor said, unbuttoning her shirt and unhooking her bra. "Right now, we've got some celebrating to do."

"Mmm," Tamara purred as his big, warm hands cupped her breasts. "Did you have anything in particular in mind?"

His eyes glinted wolfishly. "Why don't I just show you?"

Two weeks later, Victor and Tamara attended a party at the Chart House, an upscale Old Town restaurant that boasted spectacular waterfront views. The private reception was to celebrate the retirement of one of Hopewell General's most beloved surgeons.

Most of the hospital's staff was in attendance, including the newly engaged Jaclyn and Dr. De Winter, as well as Dr. Dudley and his wife, Lucille. Nurse Tsang was conspicuously absent.

Throughout the evening, Victor and Tamara accepted hearty congratulations and well wishes on their engagement, which Victor had made official by giving Tamara a beautiful princess-cut diamond ring.

Halfway through the party, they wandered outside to the terrace that overlooked the Potomac River. They stood at the balcony sipping their champagne and gazing out at the glistening dark waters, silently reflecting on the incredible journey that had brought them from bitter rivals to soul mates.

Tamara was the first to articulate the quiet sense of wonder Victor was feeling. "I can't believe how much has happened over these past several weeks."

"Neither can I," Victor murmured.

"If anyone had told me two months ago that you and I would be engaged and living together, I would have had that person committed to the mental ward."

Victor chuckled softly. "Me, too."

Tamara smiled. "Guess it just goes to show how little *we* know, huh?"

"Speak for yourself," Victor quipped. "*I* know plenty."

Tamara punched him playfully on the arm, and he laughed. "We may not be enemies anymore," he teased affectionately, "but every now and then, you know I'll have to say *something* to get a rise out of you."

She rolled her eyes in mock exasperation. "Of course."

Smiling, Victor took their champagne flutes and set them down on the balustrade, then curved his arms around Tamara's waist and pulled her close for a deep, lingering kiss that sent heat curling through his veins.

"Not that I'm not enjoying the company of our friends and colleagues," he whispered against her mouth, staring into her glittering dark eyes, "but when do you think we can cut out without appearing rude?"

"Soon," she purred, licking at the seam of his lips. When his tongue snaked out to meet hers, she added throatily, "*Very* soon."

When someone whistled at them from inside the restaurant, they drew reluctantly apart, grinning abashedly at each other.

"To be continued later," Victor promised with a wink.

"You'd better believe it." Keeping her arms looped around his neck, Tamara gazed deeply into Victor's eyes. "I love you so much. Thank you again and again for saving my mother's life, and for being every bit as amazing as she always believed you were."

Placing his hand against the warm, satiny skin above the neckline of Tamara's dress, Victor murmured huskily, "Thank *you*."

"For?"

"For allowing me to enjoy the incredible privilege of loving you." He smiled tenderly into her eyes. "And for listening to your heart."

* * * * *

REQUEST YOUR FREE BOOKS!

2 FREE NOVELS
PLUS 2 FREE GIFTS!

KIMANI™
ROMANCE

Love's ultimate destination!

YES! Please send me 2 FREE Kimani™ Romance novels and my 2 FREE gifts (gifts are worth about $10). After receiving them, if I don't wish to receive any more books, I can return the shipping statement marked "cancel." If I don't cancel, I will receive 4 brand-new novels every month and be billed just $4.94 per book in the U.S. or $5.49 per book in Canada. That's a saving of at least 21% off the cover price. It's quite a bargain! Shipping and handling is just 50¢ per book in the U.S. and 75¢ per book in Canada.* I understand that accepting the 2 free books and gifts places me under no obligation to buy anything. I can always return a shipment and cancel at any time. Even if I never buy another book, the two free books and gifts are mine to keep forever.

168/368 XDN FEJR

Name _____ (PLEASE PRINT) _____

Address _____ Apt. # _____

City _____ State/Prov. _____ Zip/Postal Code _____

Signature (if under 18, a parent or guardian must sign)

Mail to the Reader Service:
IN U.S.A.: P.O. Box 1867, Buffalo, NY 14240-1867
IN CANADA: P.O. Box 609, Fort Erie, Ontario L2A 5X3

Not valid for current subscribers to Kimani Romance books.

Want to try two free books from another line?
Call 1-800-873-8635 or visit www.ReaderService.com.

* Terms and prices subject to change without notice. Prices do not include applicable taxes. Sales tax applicable in N.Y. Canadian residents will be charged applicable taxes. Offer not valid in Quebec. This offer is limited to one order per household. All orders subject to credit approval. Credit or debit balances in a customer's account(s) may be offset by any other outstanding balance owed by or to the customer. Please allow 4 to 6 weeks for delivery. Offer available while quantities last.

Your Privacy—The Reader Service is committed to protecting your privacy. Our Privacy Policy is available online at www.ReaderService.com or upon request from the Reader Service.

We make a portion of our mailing list available to reputable third parties that offer products we believe may interest you. If you prefer that we not exchange your name with third parties, or if you wish to clarify or modify your communication preferences, please visit us at www.ReaderService.com/consumerschoice or write to us at Reader Service Preference Service, P.O. Box 9062, Buffalo, NY 14269. Include your complete name and address.

KROM11B

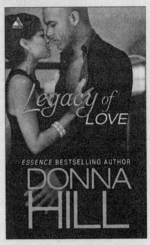